SPY DOG
STORM CHASER

You don't tend to see many 'spy pets' because, basically, they're undercover. A few bizarre animals crop up on the internet. Surfing dogs, trampolining cats, that kind of thing. I think I might even have seen a baby monkey riding on a pig? But they're not 'spies'. Because, like I said, spies are so secret that you never see them doing anything out of the ordinary.

But I thought I'd set you a challenge. Remember, just because you don't *see* spy pets doesn't mean they're not there. So, be alert. Keep your eyes peeled. In fact, be a bit of a spy yourself. If you see your pet doing anything unusual, send me a pic and I'll set up a classified file of 'spy pets'.

andy@artofbrilliance.co.uk

Books by Andrew Cope

Spy Dog series in reading order

SPY DOG

CAPTURED!

UNLEASHED!

SUPERBRAIN

ROCKET RIDER

SECRET SANTA

TEACHER'S PET

ROLLERCOASTER!

BRAINWASHED

MUMMY MADNESS

STORM CHASER

Spy Pups series in reading order

TREASURE QUEST

PRISON BREAK

CIRCUS ACT

DANGER ISLAND

SURVIVAL CAMP

Spy Cat series in reading order

SUMMER SHOCKER!

BLACKOUT!

SPY DOG JOKE BOOK

SPY DOG
STORM CHASER

ANDREW COPE
Ably and significantly assisted by Will Hussey

Illustrated by James de la Rue

PUFFIN

PUFFIN BOOKS

UK | USA | Canada | Ireland | Australia
India | New Zealand | South Africa

Puffin Books is part of the Penguin Random House group of companies whose
addresses can be found at global.penguinrandomhouse.com.

puffinbooks.com

Penguin
Random House
UK

First published 2015

001

Text copyright © Andrew Cope, 2015
Illustrations copyright © James de la Rue, 2015

The moral right of the author and illustrator has been asserted

Set in Bembo Book MT Std 15/18 pt
Typeset by Palimpsest Book Production Limited, Falkirk, Stirlingshire
Printed in Great Britain by Clays Ltd, St Ives plc

A CIP catalogue record for this book is available from the British Library

ISBN: 978-0-141-35715-7

www.greenpenguin.co.uk

For Martha and Henry: thanks for making Mondays special.

Contents

1. Ken's Invention

Fifty-five years, three months and two days ago . . .

Even by old-fashioned standards, Mr Dewitt was old-fashioned. He'd risen to head teacher by insisting things were done the right way. *His* way. It was a very simple system. He would write on the blackboard, in exaggerated loopy handwriting, and the children would copy it down. Facts mostly. And if it wasn't done properly then it had to be done all over again. 'Dewitt Again' made sure of that.

6D smelt of egg. In the winter the smell of egg was overpowering. In the summer the stench was even worse. Mr Dewitt ate egg-and-cress sandwiches for his elevenses, egg-and-cress sandwiches for his dinner and egg-and-cress sandwiches if he needed a snack in-between

times. It would be fair to say that Mr Dewitt liked egg. He also had a plentiful supply. Every morning for the past fifty years, the headmaster had wandered down to the chicken shed at the bottom of his garden, returning shortly afterwards with half a dozen freshly laid eggs. Every single day. Mr Dewitt knew a thing or two about chickens. In fact, he considered himself to be a bit of an 'egg-spert'.

In his classes there were very few questions and absolutely no nonsense. If they weren't copying things from the board, the general rule was that the children worked in silence. And if they were copying things from the board, the general rule was that the children worked in silence too. Silence ruled while he wandered between the pupils, shoes creaking, occasionally walloping his ruler on to the desk if a child appeared to be slacking.

Which is why he loved his two top students, Maximus and Kenneth. No ruler was required. In a lifetime of teaching, he had never known ten-year-olds with such keen minds; brain-boxes that soaked up information. For him, Maximus and Kenneth were proof that copying from the board was the way forward. After all, if it worked for them, then it should work for everyone. Even better, the boys seemed to spur each other on, both trying to be top of the class. They excelled across the board – if you discounted sport, that is; they preferred to exercise their brains instead. Maximus was slightly chubby and insisted on keeping his white lab coat on, even in PE. He'd recently received a football in the face and his spectacles were held together with a sticking plaster provided by matron. Kenneth, on the other hand, was tall and gangly. Although he looked built for long-distance running, he often struggled to coordinate his limbs and found himself spreadeagled on the track. He was a running joke.

But what the boys lacked in PE, they made up for in mathematics and science. And here they were, about to demonstrate their skills at the esteemed end-of-year head-to-head 'show-and-tell'. Mr Dewitt believed in competition. He'd drummed it into the children that taking part was for wimps. It was the winning that mattered. Kenneth and Maximus had spent the entire Year 5 working on their own top-secret science project that they were about to demonstrate to the class.

A slightly nervous Kenneth was up first. 'Ah-hem,' he began, clearing his throat. There followed a long pause. Everything about Kenneth was long. His long, slender fingers led to overgrown, yellowing fingernails that tapped impatiently on everything he touched. A slightly crooked nose seemed to protrude from the middle of his pimpled forehead and continue down to a thin, pointy chin. Even his own mother probably wouldn't have considered him a 'looker', even if she had really bad eyesight. His nostrils flared with every breath, accompanied by a high-pitched whistling as the air was sucked all the way up. A steady stream of snot continually oozed out; only to be licked from his top lip by a long, lizard-like tongue.

'Thank you, sir, for allowing me to address the class,' he blurted at last.

Mr Dewitt nodded. 'Get on with it, laddie,' he said. 'It's sports day, so we all want to be outside.' In other words, Mr Dewitt wanted to be outside.

'Err . . . Yes, sir. As you can see, I have written a few ideas on the board behind me.'

Forty children gasped at the series of diagrams and equations that filled the entire blackboard. All looked completely bemused, except young Maximus, who sat nodding appreciatively. *Chemical imbalances in the barometric pressure of the atmosphere. Impressive.* He knew the bar was set high.

'I have been investigating the atmosphere,'

announced Kenneth. He turned to an object on Mr Dewitt's desk and whipped off the tea towel, revealing a small metal dish with an antenna. 'This is my Climacta-sphere 1960.' Mr Dewitt's left eye twitched: he didn't like surprises. Unless he had agreed to them first, of course.

Kenneth was encouraged to hear someone stifle a 'Golly gosh'. He continued with renewed confidence.

'The Climacta-sphere 1960 shoots particles

6

into the sky.' He paused for effect, eyes darting around the room. 'And I have found a secret ingredient that has the power to change the weather.'

There was an audible 'Wow!' among Kenneth's classmates. The headmaster twitched again. Emily's hand shot up. Mr Dewitt trusted Emily to ask a good question, so he nodded approvingly.

'Wowee! So you can create sunshine!' she beamed. 'You can make it so we don't have dreary grey days?'

There was a pause as Kenneth's feet shifted awkwardly and he looked away. 'My experiments are in the early stages,' he mumbled through his nose. 'At the moment, I can create the opposite. As you know, my father owns a chicken farm and I've harnessed the power of chicken waste to create clouds.' He extended a bony finger, pointing at the left-hand side of the board. 'This is how it works.'

His audience looked on, goggle-eyed at the jigsaw of chalked numbers and letters. 'Small scale at the moment,' he admitted with a shrug. 'You might have noticed, I've managed to create a cloud at home?'

Forty pairs of eyes grew wider still as they tried to picture the eerie farm on the hill above the town. It sure was dark and thundery up there. Come to think of it, the farm was almost always hidden behind a cloud these days. Emily's hand shot up once more. She got the nod. 'I don't get it,' she said. 'What's the point of dark, grey clouds when you could have nice blue sky?'

Kenneth Soop's mouth opened but no words came out. He was devastated. Emily – wonderful Emily, the light of his life, the girl he admired from afar – didn't get it. What's more, she was putting the boot into his invention. *Emily didn't like it* . . . His droopy shoulders slumped and his long nose pointed to the floor as he heard the other children mumbling in agreement. Kenneth was only ten years old but he already knew he was different. He loved darkness and clouds. He'd recently experimented with adding more of his secret formula and his hilltop farm had enjoyed thunder and lightning for a whole week. He'd sat in his bedroom gazing through the storm at the sunny town below and had never felt happier. He just didn't understand why everyone else seemed to like gloriously hot, sunny days. For Kenneth, grey was the new blue.

'A jolly good effort,' congratulated Mr Dewitt, not sounding particularly jolly. 'A secret ingredient that changes the weather is, indeed, of considerable scientific importance. Maybe just needs a little refinement before it's ready to go,' he barked, with a twitch.

Young Kenneth tried not to sag on the outside but part of him was shrivelling on the inside. His classmates didn't get it. Mr Dewitt didn't get it. He blinked back hot tears and the urge to run and hide. One day, he vowed, everyone would realize just how valuable a dark cloud could be.

'Next up,' prompted the head teacher, nodding to the ten-year-old in a white lab coat, 'young Maximus Cortex.'

2. Hoody v. Doggie

Today . . .

It was far too hot for wearing a hoody, but the boy's hood was up and his trousers were slung impossibly low, revealing the make of his grubby pink boxer shorts as he sped around the BMX track. Brickfield Town park was just around the corner from the local primary school and kids of all ages enjoyed hurtling around the bends and flying over the dirt humps. Most of the time.

Children spluttered as the hoody tore past, kicking choking plumes of dust in their faces and scattering the other bikes from the track. He was much bigger than anyone else and obviously liked to throw his weight around. Ollie Cook looked on nervously. It was his first time at the track and he'd been looking forward to trying out his brand new birthday present: a shiny red dirt-bike complete with front and rear stunt pegs. The jumps looked a lot bigger close up, and looking at the hoody he didn't feel quite so confident any more.

Ollie wasn't yet old enough to go to the park by himself. Sometimes his big brother Ben would let him tag along, but today he was having trials for the area football team. His older sister Sophie would have taken him if she could, but she'd been invited to go to the cinema for a friend's birthday treat. Dad had driven Ben to the trials and Mum was working this afternoon; she was doing an extra shift at the hospital. Ollie didn't mind, though, because he had Lara, otherwise known as GM451, the world's number one retired Spy Dog. Lara was like a best friend, parent and sister rolled into one. Shakespeare, the Cook family's pet cat would have come too but he was currently being put through his paces with the SAS (Special Animal Service) refining his survival skills – having already used up the majority of his nine lives. And of course there were Spud and Star, Lara's pups, who were always up for a bit of adventure . . .

The pups sat on top of the slide overlooking the track, giving them a grandstand view. The black one with a slightly podgy tummy gave a low growl and got to his paws. 'That boy in the hoody is doing his best to get in everyone's way. He's going to cause an accident . . .'

'Relax, bro,' soothed his sister, 'we've got it covered. Besides, technically it wouldn't be an accident if it was deliberate.' Star smiled; even though she could only bark English, she was pretty good with words. Star was slightly taller than her brother and had inherited her mother's black and white patches. Spud sat back down. Out of the corner of his eye he spotted the village ice-cream van approaching, which immediately made him cheer up a bit. *Hmmm . . . Where's Mum?* With a bit of luck she'd have a few spare pennies for emergencies. Like needing an ice cream.

Ollie gripped his handlebars and pushed off with a slight wobble. A little shakily, he managed to get his pedals turning and headed for the next jump. He had a good line and knew that he could do it if he really concentrated. 'Here goes,' he said aloud to himself as he reached the top of the slope, before plummeting down to gather speed. Faster and faster he went, gritting his teeth as the wind made his eyes water. Ollie was just about to pull the handlebars towards him on the cusp of the jump, when the hoody careered past, knocking him off-balance and making him veer wildly to the left.

'Aaaaargh!' screamed Ollie, holding on for all he was worth and struggling to keep his balance. His brand-new bike bucked like a wild horse as his front tyre hit a pothole, throwing its rider, who somersaulted through the air. Spud and Star were already on their way, skidding on two paws down the slide before hitting the ground running.

Ollie turned a full circle in the air and landed flat on his back in the sandpit with an 'Ooof!' Star was the first to reach him, and immediately began running through a series of first-aid assessments. As a trained paramedic she automatically checked Ollie's vital signs: *Pulse rate, breathing, temperature, any fractures?*

'How's my bike?' wheezed Ollie. 'Is it still shiny?' *Sounds like he's OK, just a few bumps and scratches. Good job he was wearing a helmet!* Star gave him a reassuring lick.

Spud wandered over to inspect the damage to Ollie's new bike. The back wheel was still spinning. The front wheel was horribly buckled where it had struck the pothole and there was now a long, jagged scratch on the paintwork. 'Err . . . It just needs fixing up a little,' he barked, hoping to lessen the blow. Ollie sat up gingerly and stared at his bike. He quickly looked away again, trying to blink away the tears.

The hoody was now positioned back at the start line, slumped over his bike, resting his elbows on the crossbar. This was his track, and everyone needed to remember that. If some kid was daft enough to get in the way, then they got what they deserved. He removed his hood to reveal a round, pink face with chubby red cheeks. His hair was cut short and he gave the impression of being a little too big for his bike. Tufts of hair protruded through the gaps in his cycle helmet, making him look a little like a skunk. Star thought he smelt like one too.

Spud was on his paws barking furiously at the hoody. *He needs to learn some respect! And he needs to pull his trousers up. Grrrrr!*

'Wait.' Star gently placed a restraining paw upon her brother, 'Look.' Sidling seemingly out of nowhere a black and white dog pedalled up alongside the big boy on the small bike. Lara removed her full-face helmet with two paws and turned to fix her attention on the hoody. She raised one ear in consternation, the late-afternoon sun shining through a small penny-sized hole. The challenge was clear.

Lara surveyed the twists and turns of the BMX track and thought it mirrored her life perfectly. She'd had a few ups and down during her time as the world's first Spy Dog; that was before she had stumbled upon the Cook family. Ollie, Sophie and Ben had put her on the right path, and made her realize how special it was to be part of a family. She still did her bit to save the world, but these days the children always came first. If they ever needed a helping paw, then Lara would be there. Like now, for instance . . .

The skunk-boy had never seen a dog on a bike before, and had certainly never raced one. Despite that, he looked the dog up and down and decided she couldn't be too hard to beat; this mutt was obviously some way past its best. With a smirk he replaced his hood before spitting a large globule of phlegm that landed in the dust just inches from Lara's paw. *Disgusting*, thought Lara. *I'm going to have to teach this kid some manners*. She replaced her helmet and carefully secured it with her chin strap. Lara turned to signal the start of the lap, but the hoody wasn't going to wait. He powered down the ramp, sneaking a valuable few metres' advantage. While her legs weren't quite as quick as they used to be, Lara's mind was as sharp as ever. She reacted quickly and rocketed down the ramp in hot pursuit.

The hoody was clearly heavier than Lara, enabling him to build up plenty of momentum, but he was also wider. *If I can just get a bit closer, then I should be able to slipstream his wide bottom*. Lara managed to draw in close behind the hoody's rear wheel, which sheltered her from the air rushing past. *I knew Professor Cortex's astro-physics lessons would come in handy at some point*. A steep banking ahead outlined a tight turn. Lara saw her chance. *I need to stay low; I might be in with a chance of under-taking him.*

Ollie, Spud and Star watched, fixated by the action developing in front of them. 'I can't look,' whimpered Star. Spud had already covered his eyes with both paws. Ollie wiped the last few tears from his cheeks, 'GO, LARA!' he shouted. He knew how special she was – far more valuable than any bike.

Lara put her head down and steered into the corner, both of them emerging neck and neck. The finish line was in sight. The hoody was

sweating profusely and his trousers seemed to be inching lower as he battled against the panting pooch. Both riders hit the next jump simultaneously and sailed into the air; Lara couldn't resist a stylish flick of her back wheel before they both hit the ground again.

The hoody was starting to panic now. Lara was edging into the lead, and he was in danger of losing face as well as his trousers. He swerved into the path of the dog, almost barging her off the track. 'HEY!' shouted Ollie, who couldn't believe anyone would stoop so low. Spud and Star exchanged a nervous glance. They knew their Mum could handle herself, but then again, she wasn't getting any younger . . .

Lara somehow managed to keep her BMX on track, throwing her hind legs to one side to regain her balance. The hoody could see that she was in trouble and prepared to knock her clean off this time. He put his head down and headed straight for Lara once again. 'Yikes! She's got nowhere to go!' yelped Spud.

Fortunately Lara was no ordinary dog. As a highly trained secret agent, she was used to coping with situations such as these, remaining calm and making split-second decisions under pressure. *Gotta think clearly and act fast. Hmmm, less is sometimes more.* At the very last moment, before the hoody made contact, Lara slammed on her brakes. Missing her by inches, the skunk hurtled off the edge of the track and smashed through the surrounding wooden fencing. Shortly afterwards there was a considerable *SPLASH!* followed by the angry quacking of some displaced ducks.

Lara, Ollie and the pups all raced round to the duck pond where there appeared to be a new water feature – wearing a hoody. Star began laughing; the sight of the boy standing knee-deep in water with his trousers around his ankles was extremely funny. Lara shook her head; she knew that the boy had escaped lightly – it was only his pride that had been hurt. The familiar chimes of the ice-cream van drifted over to them.

The four of them made their way home, enjoying an ice cream in the hazy sunshine and taking it in turn to push Ollie's damaged bike. He was upset and perhaps a little worried at what Mum might say, but Lara had tried to reassure him. 'Spud will take care of your bike,' she barked, throwing her son a look. 'I will? Yes, I mean – *I will*,' barked the chunky black pup.

No one noticed the dark black cloud that was beginning to form on the early evening horizon. It was a very dark cloud on a very bright day and looked more than a little out of place. The birds stopped singing and headed for shelter high up in the trees. The temperature dropped noticeably as a large shadow seeped over the park. The calm was over. It was time for the storm.

Far from anywhere, on a remote hill top, Ken Soop was smiling. His new improved Climacta-sphere 2015 was working.

3. Hot Stuff

Fifty-five years, three months and two days earlier . . .

Young Maximus Cortex lived for science. He was a geek of the highest order but, as lovely Emily had pointed out, 'That's what makes Max special.' He was better with animals than people and his dog was the only one in the neighbourhood that had a built-in collar light for night-time walkies. He'd been terrifically impressed by Kenneth's idea and had even jotted a few notes during his classmate's presentation. Now it came to his turn and he was feeling flustered. Science was his thing. Public speaking most definitely wasn't. Words made more sense inside his head than out. The young scientist brushed his clammy hands down his lab coat, straightening it and breathing deeply for confidence.

'Thank you, Kenneth,' he began. 'I think you'll find that you can reverse the polarity of your invention to create sunshine,' he said helpfully. He walked over to the board and smudged out one of the chemical symbols, scribbling $4H_kQ^{97}$ in its place. 'See? Bright, huh? Maybe we can work on it together?'

Kenneth Soop smiled weakly. There was not a cat-in-hell's chance.

'I have several inventions on the go this year,' announced Maximus. 'I'm working on something that's like a web of information, but worldwide. I've code named it "The Interesting Net". Or I might shorten it to "The Internet"?' he thought aloud. 'It will allow you to access information on anything in the world at any time. Instantly.'

The class gasped. Mr Dewitt twitched, looking horrified. *He* was the font of all wisdom, so Maximus moved swiftly on. 'But this is my personal favourite.' He left the room momentarily before wheeling in a squeaky trolley. A large metal box rested on the top. The box had a window in the front and a series of dials and knobs. The class waited patiently while Maximus plugged the box into the socket beside Mr Dewitt's desk. He stood and proudly wafted his hands across the machine. 'I call it the "Dinner-Meister2000".'

'What does it do?' asked Frank, unable to conceal his excitement.

'Well,' began Maximus, 'if you press this button here, a door opens,' he demonstrated, the front of the box opening up. 'And you pop food inside.'

'Like a safe, but for food?' guessed Emily. 'It's brilliant!'

Maximus smiled. He went to the blackboard and drew a diagram. 'Normal cooking,' he began, 'starts on the outside and works inwards. So, for example, you put a cake in the oven and it warms up on the outside, with the inside cooking last.'

Maximus Cortex peered over the sticking plaster on his spectacles at the confused faces in class 5A.

'And that's rather inefficient,' he explained. 'So I've been experimenting with smaller waves of energy that will cook food much faster, because it starts cooking on the *inside*.' He'd drawn a round object with arrows coming out of it, like some sort of explosion. 'I call them "micro-waves",' beamed Maximus.

'So that's a *micro-wave* oven?' guessed Emily.

'That's an excellent name for it, Emily,' he said, scribbling the name on a pad. 'Very catchy. Shall I show you how it works?'

His classmates were nodding enthusiastically. 'Has anyone got any food that needs cooking or warming up?'

All eyes fell on Kenneth Soop. He was the only one who didn't have school dinners. Every day he brought a flask of cold soup. He seemed to prefer it cold, but surely there was no harm in warming it up.

'Kenneth, please let Maximus have your flask,' beckoned a curious Mr Dewitt, not about to offer his egg-and-cress sandwiches. The lanky youth rummaged in his school bag before reluctantly handing over a flask. Maximus unscrewed the lid and poured the grey liquid into a dish. He gagged at the smell but politely carried on. 'Cold soup goes in,' explained Maximus. He turned a knob and twisted a dial before pressing a big red button on the top of the machine. There was a whirring noise and everyone peered into the window as the dish started rotating. Thirty seconds later, the machine pinged and Maximus opened the door. 'And . . . *ta-da!* . . . Piping-hot soup comes out, *ouch*!' he said, scalding his fingers on Kenneth's soup.

There was a spontaneous round of applause as Kenneth peered into his instantly hot broth.

'This is just an early prototype,' explained the ten-year-old. 'Eventually I see the whole world using' – he glanced down at his notepad – '*micro-waved* meals. Maybe companies will start producing dinners that are designed especially for *micro-wave ovens?* Instant meals. You could even do a Sunday dinner that's *micro-waveable.*'

The class were in hysterics. Mr Dewitt snorted loudly. He knew that it took his wife all of Sunday morning to cook his Sunday roast. 'You and your imagination, Maximus,' he scoffed.

Mr Dewitt reminded the children that it was the winning that mattered before the class voted on the best invention. Emily thought about voting for Kenneth's Climacta-sphere 1960 purely out of sympathy. But black clouds seemed like such a bad idea so she went with the unanimous vote.

'Smile for the camera,' snapped Mr Dewitt, disappearing under a black hood and pulling a cord. The timer counted down as the head teacher reappeared and hastily positioned himself behind the two boys. 'The winner and loser together,' he declared as the camera flashed. Maximus Cortex's spectacles were as wonky as his grin. Kenneth Soop's eyes were as thunderous as his invention.

The school dinner hall was alive with excited chatter. Children were taking it in turns to put their puddings into the newly named 'micro-wave oven', marvelling at the instant heat.

'Remember I was the one who came up with the name,' blushed Emily.

Kenneth Soop sat alone in the classroom. He'd thrown his hot soup away. He hated hot soup. He hated Maximus Cortex. But most of all he hated people. He shook his flask to check there was something left within. Unscrewing the top of the flask he removed the lid. The smell immediately engulfed the classroom like a pungent fog. Kenneth Soop waited a moment, eyes closed, the edges of his mouth almost smiling as he savoured the horrible aroma. After a minute he tipped the flask to reveal a revolting grey sludge that spattered the surrounding table top. He lifted the cup to his nose and inhaled deeply, before taking a large gulp of the grisly contents, some of which escaped down his chin.

He glanced out at the summer's day and remembered there was something he hated even more than happy people. *Sports Day!* The ten-year-old boy glanced out into the corridor to check the coast was clear before lifting his Climacta-sphere 1960 on to the desk at the back of the classroom. He plugged it in and opened the window. He pressed the button and his invention throbbed with energy. A bolt of lightning ripped into the blue sky and sixty seconds later dark clouds gathered over the school and large drops of rain smattered against the window. The whistle blew and the children ran indoors for a wet playtime.

Ken Soop's mouth turned upwards. Sports Day was cancelled. *Now who's the winner?* Grey days made him happy. It seemed every cloud had a silver lining.

4. The Cloud Maker

Today . . .

Ben, Sophie and Ollie were hungry as usual, so Mum was putting together some snacks. The TV news was delivering its usual negativity in the background. There seemed to be an awful lot of 'chicken' news. Mum pointed the remote control at the screen and pressed the volume button. Sales of chicken soup were at an all-time high and there had been a spate of chicken stealing. The reporter was wearing her best concerned look whilst struggling to take the missing chickens story seriously. 'Police are puzzled,' she said. 'They are eggs-amining the evidence as I speak.' Dad let out a laugh while tying his laces; Ben didn't think it was that funny. He wondered if it was just a coincidence that the more tins of chicken soup disappeared off the supermarket shelves, the more chickens mysteriously vanished. *Maybe not.* Ben looked out of the window. He noticed blue sky above, but there was a dark cloud on the horizon. The cloud matched his thoughts. Ben furrowed his brow; something didn't quite add up.

Dad finished his stretching and did an energetic sprint on the spot. 'It's such a beautiful day, I've decided to go for a jog.'

Lara wagged her tail hard. *And as your personal trainer, it's a great way to combine walkies with getting fit.*

'But there's rain coming,' noted Ben, pointing at the dark horizon.

'Don't be silly,' said Dad, puffing out his chest as he opened the front door. 'I watched the weather forecast and the lady said it's set to be fair for the week! Big yellow sunshines all over the UK! Hurrah!'

'I used to be a head teacher, you know,' clipped the wrinkly old man. 'In the days when schools were proper places of learning. There was no nonsense in my classroom. We had discipline.

I had respect. Pupils did it my way: Mr Dewitt's way.' His left eye twitched.

The care assistant didn't seem to care very much and she certainly didn't have time to 'Dewitt' his way. She popped one of old Mr Dewitt's chocolates into her mouth before disappearing into the sunshine. The head teacher thought back to his school days; teachers and pupils would stand up smartly when he walked into the classroom. He used to be somebody back then.

In Bleak House Nursing Home he was just another one of the residents; they didn't even call him 'sir'. He watched the care assistant pegging the off-white sheets to the washing line; it wouldn't take long for them to dry today. He'd show them. *He still was somebody . . .*

Suddenly, as if from nowhere, a dark cloud cast its shadow across the lawn. There was a flash of lightning and a crack of thunder, before the rain began to pour. In the commotion that followed, no one noticed the long, slender fingers tapping on old Mr Dewitt's window. The head teacher smiled thinly and shuffled over to unlock the catch. Peering out, his gaze was met by the long, slender features of Kenneth Soop.

'Greetings, my dear boy. I understand you
are in need of my expertise?'

Soop smiled and handed the old man a small
package wrapped in tin foil. Mr Dewitt
unwrapped it eagerly, pausing just a moment

before taking several large bites. The smell of egg sandwiches filled the room.

'Chicken business, sir. I knew you were the man to ask,' replied Soop, looking around.

'Delighted to be of assistance, my boy,' replied the ageing head teacher, spitting out small pieces of egg. The world was about to Dewitt his way once again . . .

Mr Cook was trying to go faster, but his gut seemed to disagree with his feet. It had been a beautiful summer's day when he had set out for his jog, but Ben had been right, there was now a threatening black cloud that had appeared from nowhere. Lara, his newly appointed personal trainer, skipped effortlessly alongside him, barking words of encouragement. *Keep it up, Mr C! Remember: no pain, no gain . . .*

Lara had designed him a training plan to try to shed a few pounds. Mr Cook had been a good runner in his schooldays and had even won a few races. That all seemed a long time ago now, as he struggled to outrun the impending deluge. *Almost there, Mr C; you could be on for a personal best time!*

They finally reached the front garden gate.
Mr Cook was soaked. He shuffled along the
path slightly pigeon-toed, with his hands on
hips, before collapsing through the front door.
Lara clasped a pencil between her teeth. Using
the blunt end, she recorded today's time on Mr
Cook's tablet, making sure she kept track of
his daily progress. *Pretty good, Mr C – that's a
whole minute faster than yesterday!* Ollie bounded

down the stairs on hearing their return and threw his Dad a towel. 'Wow, Dad! You look shattered!'

'Thanks,' puffed Mr Cook. 'Blooming weather lady got it very wrong, though. I had to sprint the last half-mile to get out of the storm!'

Overhead, the black cloud seemed to be increasing in size. Blocking out the sunlight, it cast a dark shadow that fell over the Cooks' street and much of the surrounding neighbourhood. Rain continued to fall, softly at first, then hammering down upon the pavements and rooftops. Anyone unlucky enough to be caught outside soon made their way inside to shelter from the storm. The temperature dropped.

Mr Cook, showered and ruddy-faced after his jog, sat in his favourite armchair, his attention fixed on the news. 'Look at that weather map!' he said, gesticulating at the screen. 'The rest of the country has blue sky and sunshine and our little town has a permanent black cloud. It's just not fair!'

Outside, a single chicken feather fell softly from the skies above.

5. Secret Snot

Kenneth Soop's long, pale, skeletal fingers gave way to similarly long, yellow fingernails. They flicked between the Great Dane's ears, rehoming a few resident fleas. The guard dog smiled; a scratch from his master was praise indeed.

The master was pleased – although he didn't show it. Ken Soop removed his fingers from the dog's head and inserted one extraordinarily long digit up his extraordinarily long ski-jump nose. He rummaged around for a moment, before removing something sticky from the depths of his left nostril. He peered at it distractedly, before replacing it in his right nostril. Soop's moist moustache twitched, his thin lips causing it to ripple like a shuffling caterpillar. It had taken nearly sixty years, but he had finally found a way of spreading the unhappiness. The moment had arrived.

The warehouse was vast, but the Cloud Maker seemed to fill it. A ring of churning vats surrounded complicated machinery with endless flashing lights and levers. In the centre of it all, what looked like a large, black satellite dish pointed towards the glass-domed ceiling.

Soop looked around at his team of one: his former head teacher. Mr Dewitt was nearly ninety but wasn't finished yet. The old man knew a thing or two about chickens and seemed keen to prove he could still 'Dewitt'. Of course, this time Mr Dewitt would have to 'do it' Kenneth's way. 'If you please, sir.' After a second nod, the retired headmaster grasped a lever and pulled down. There was a great deal of whirring and clicking as the great glass roof began to retract, revealing the bright blue sky above. The enormous guard dogs, Mr Heinz and Mr Campbell, looked on.

The tall, spindly frame of Ken Soop wandered over to a large red button, his black trousers and polo neck further emphasizing his lanky limbs. Both hands hovered momentarily above the knob, fingers interlocked, before Soop activated the Cloud Maker.

Crackling streaks of black lightning shot out of the centre of the satellite dish, filling the sky with a thick, dark smog. Static electricity charged the air; Mr Dewitt's comb-over twitched, the dogs' fur stood on end and Soop's jumper sizzled. The smell of burnt chicken snot filled the warehouse.

The rain was almost immediate. Everything was going according to plan. The Cloud Maker was fully functional and the summer sunshine had been snuffed out all over town. Soop laughed, enjoying the fact that it wouldn't be long before the whole town would be feeling utterly miserable; they deserved it.

Next to the warehouse containing the Cloud Maker was another equally large building. As Soop approached, he could hear a loud commotion of clucking and squawking. Pushing open the corrugated door, he was faced with line upon line, row upon row, of chickens of every shape, size and colour. Mr Dewitt was parading along the first line of chickens, checking that all was in order. Each bird had a tray of feed in front of it. He picked up a handful of seed from the nearest and held it up to examine more closely. The seed was mixed in with black peppercorns. Dewitt sniffed deeply before sneezing loudly – causing the amount of clucking to escalate even further. He bent his long, thin school cane menacingly; the old teacher had always known how to get the most out of chickens.

All along the rows the captive chickens were pecking the feed and sneezing, the expelled contents captured in a plastic funnel positioned in front of them. Each funnel was channelled into what looked like a drainpipe, from which the murky, sticky liquid was then collected in a sizeable barrel at the end of the row.

'Who'd have thought it? Chicken snot. The secret weather-changing ingredient,' breathed Soop sinisterly. It was time for the second phase of the operation. 'I created the problem,' he purred, 'and I just happen to have the solution!' If that wasn't evil genius, he didn't know what was.

Stepping out of the warehouse, an enormous

truck idled on the forecourt, its engine growling noisily, with thick plumes of diesel smoke belching into the sky. The monster lorry had darkened tinted windows in the cab, shrouding the identity of the driver, but the huge letters on the side of the wagon gave a big clue: *KEN SOOP'S CHICKEN SOUP.*

Nodding in appreciation of his own evil brilliance, Ken Soop wandered to the truck and opened the passenger door. 'Up you go, Mr Campbell,' he said. 'And you too, Mr Heinz.'

The Great Danes leapt into the cab, leaving a trail of slobber, before Ken Soop slammed the door. He walked round to the driver's door and hauled himself aboard. He revved the engine, revelling in the power of the throaty roar. This was to be the third delivery and Ken Soop wanted to make sure it was done properly. So: he was in control, he'd invented the soup, he'd made the soup, he'd canned the soup and he was now delivering the soup. In fact, he was a total control freak. The only other person who knew of the plan was Mr Dewitt, but he just wanted to be noticed again; that and an endless supply of egg sandwiches.

★

Ollie was fed up. He wanted to go outside but the rain had been pouring non-stop for two days now. He liked to take shots at Lara – she was quite a handy goalkeeper. Alas, Mrs Cook had said 'no'. She didn't want to deal with a trail of muddy kit.

Mr Cook sat in the kitchen reading the newspaper. He'd not managed to get out for a jog in this weather – a little rain was OK, but not a downpour.

'Well, at least you won't lose much fitness,' Ben had chimed rather unkindly. 'You weren't very fast to begin with.' Mr Cook had taken offence at this and decided to confiscate the computer console – which Sophie had just happened to be playing on at the time.

'That's not fair, Dad!' she exclaimed. It wasn't long before all three children were sitting in their rooms in a huff.

Lara sat in the conservatory, meditating. Her legs were crossed in the lotus position and paws clasped in front, helping to clear her thoughts. Around her, Spud and Star bickered.

'A Spy Dog needs brains,' Spud yowled at his sister, 'any old dog can learn a few tricks.'

'I guess that counts you out then,' retorted

Star, scowling at her brother, 'because you're always barking up the wrong tree . . .'

Lara slowly opened one eye. Amidst the commotion she could hear the rain clattering against the plastic roof. *That cloud hasn't moved for two whole days and this is supposed to be summer. The Cooks' home is normally such a happy house-hold. Something's not right . . .*

6. Feeling Flushed

The rain still hammering down, Ollie had resorted to playing with the craft set he had received last Christmas. He was actually quite enjoying it, and was currently sticking the sequins and feathers on to a piece of red card with rather a lot of glue. It held together OK, but unfortunately seemed to be firmly attached to the bedroom carpet. He frowned.

Everyone in the Cook house was feeling a bit down in the dumps.

'I know,' ventured Mum, 'I fancy some of that Soop's Chicken Soup. That'll make us feel better – it always does.'

Dad wasn't convinced, but decided better than to comment. Sophie and Ben both wanted a takeaway, but then again, Sophie and Ben always wanted a takeaway.

Mum opened the kitchen cupboard.

'Oh, we've run out. I'll have to get some more.'

'Oh – woof,' Lara was already at the front door, signalling to the pups. *We'll go. It'll give me a chance to investigate.*

'We will?' spluttered Spud, looking at the weather with his tail between his legs. Lara gave him a look which said it all.

While the rain had abated a little, the dark black cloud still loomed ominously above them. Lara trotted along the pavement flanked by Star and Spud, the latter wearing his MP3 headphones and strutting slightly. Brickfield was usually a fun and friendly place to live, but today it felt pretty miserable. The people they passed didn't smile or acknowledge them, but instead hurried about their business with their heads down. *Strange,* thought Lara. *There really is a cloud hanging over everyone.*

When they finally reached the supermarket, it was pandemonium. Large queues had formed at the tills, with people jostling each other for position. Shoppers stood with arms, trolleys and baskets crammed full of tins of Ken Soop's Chicken Soup, completely jamming the aisles.

One man accidentally dropped a tin, which was immediately pounced on by a lady with a pushchair and another man who had arrived a minute ago by mobility scooter. A short scuffle ensued, the lady with the pushchair emerging victorious with the (slightly dented) tin of soup.

By now the slightly panicky store manager had appeared attempting to calm the situation.

'Ladies and gentlemen, please. We have other varieties on the shelf.'

'We don't want any other make,' yelled a lady. 'We want Soop's soup. It's the best. My daughter won't eat anything else!'

'Then please be patient, madam,' urged the store manager. 'We're due to receive another delivery of chicken soup any minute – please rest assured there'll be enough for everyone.' The announcement just seemed to further inflame the situation, as the public braced themselves for a battle over the next batch.

'Are we going to wait for some, Ma?' enquired Spud, starting to feel decidedly uneasy.

'No, son. I don't think we will. Chicken soup's supposed to make you feel better, and I'm not sensing much of a feel-good factor right this minute.'

The dogs left the supermarket commotion empty-pawed and began the journey back home. *It'll just have to be smiley faces for dinner.*

At that moment Kenneth Soop manoeuvred his enormous truck around the corner of Brickfield High Street and headed for the supermarket. He glanced through the tinted window at the three dogs walking by and deliberately steered his truck slightly to one side in order to splash them with a large, muddy puddle. Mr Campbell and Mr Heinz approved, wagging their tails hard, swishing their boss in the face. Chuckling, Soop checked in his side-mirror. All three were soaked from head to paw. *Serves them right, looks like they needed a good shower anyway – mucky pups!*

Lara, Spud and Star all stood dripping wet, trying to make sense of what had just happened. The spy trio looked as sick as a dog. Even Spud seemed to have temporarily lost some of his swagger.

Lara read the name on the side of the truck: *Kenneth Soop* – the very same name that was causing all the fuss in the supermarket. GM451 was experienced enough to sense it wasn't just a coincidence. When there was bad stuff going down, there was usually a baddie going around . . .

Lara turned to Star.

'Do you think you could snap the driver's mugshot? Something tells me it might help us to shed a little light on what's going on and who's behind it.'

The truck had momentarily halted at the traffic lights down the road, but Star knew they could change at any minute. She sprinted a dozen steps along the pavement before completing a triple somersault that left her swinging from the top of an overhanging lamppost. After a couple of rotations to increase her forward momentum, she leapt on to the branch of a nearby tree before leaping on to the roof of a handily placed four-wheel drive. A couple of athletic cat-style leaps on to neighbouring cars brought her level with the lorry's tinted cab, just as the lights began to change. A not-so-athletic nearby cat raised its eyebrows. Star twisted the tag on her collar around and pressed it three times. The collar-cam flashed, illuminating the driver for a split second.

'Not bad,' acknowledged Spud casually on his sister's return.

Lara turned to Star.

'Forward the pics to Professor Cortex ASAP. Come on, let's go.' She took three steps forward before stopping and turning. 'Oh – and well done, you two,' she winked.

Lara and the twins split up on the return journey. GM451 had someone she needed to see. The twins continued home empty-handed to report the soup shenanigans, while Lara made certain she wasn't being followed, doubling back a couple of times. When she was satisfied, she discreetly made her way across the village to the site of the new residential building development – or more specifically, the blue, plastic portable toilet cubicle adjacent to the skip. Lara waited for a minute – three to be exact. Just as she suspected, a large gentleman wearing a yellow hardhat emerged carrying a magazine. Checking the coast was clear, she darted over. Bracing herself, she opened the door and stepped inside. *Ughh! Surely builders could use air freshener!*

Holding her nose, Lara sat down on the toilet seat and engaged the door. She knew that the concealed entrance was activated by her exact body weight and waited expectantly. Nothing happened. Lara sighed. *Not again, this is so embarrassing!* She obviously weighed a fraction too much. Concentrating for a moment on the rain trickling down outside, she managed to squeeze out a small wee before washing her paws and sitting down again. Evidently she was slightly lighter this time, as the 'special flush' was activated and Lara found herself spiralling down a familiar underground water chute leading to one of Professor Cortex's top-secret underground laboratories.

Lara came to a halt, cushioned by a large, plush, purple pillow, which automatically activated several hair-dryers trained in her direction. When she looked up, the professor was standing over her.

'Ah, GM451, I've been expecting you. What took you so long?' he quizzed, before turning about and heading in the direction of his laboratory.

Nice to see you, too, Prof, thought Lara, before following with just a hint of trepidation. The professor walked over to a large white table where two test tubes stood supported by vertical clamps.

'We have a serious situation, GM451,' he said

gravely. 'A situation that I can't quite piece together.'

He bent over the test tubes, peering closely at both of them, the murky contents magnifying his slightly bloodshot left eye.

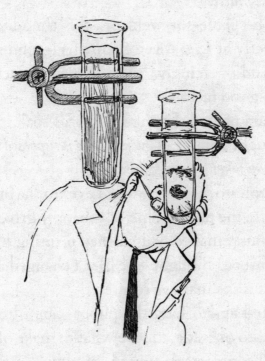

'The first contains a sample of rainwater collected from the storm cloud that's been hanging over the town.'

Lara raised her eyebrows. *OK, so what's the big deal?*

The professor continued. 'The second contains a sample of the chicken soup that currently seems to be in such demand.'

Lara looked at him. She was starting to see where he was going with this. *Are the two somehow connected?*

The professor went on, this time looking directly at Lara, 'Ken Soop's feel-good soup,' he said unerringly. 'Doesn't create much of a feel-good factor.'

Lara paused, letting the words soak in. *Yes,* thought Lara . . . *Chicken soup is supposed to pick you up when you're feeling down.*

Professor Cortex walked over to the printer, where the photograph of the lorry driver Star had just emailed had finished printing out.

'Just as I thought – he hasn't changed much. This is the man we're after.'

He handed Lara the photo. She tilted her head to one side, unsure what to make of him.

The professor smiled, reading Lara's expression.

'Kenneth and I go back a very long way. He is no *ordinary* gentleman. In fact, he is no gentleman. And this is no *ordinary* weather. And this is no *ordinary* chicken soup.'

Lara looked at the professor, waiting for him to explain further. *C'mon, Prof – spill the beans.*

'I'll start with the rain,' said the professor, picking up the test tube and gently flicking the bottom of it to cause a stir. 'It is ninety-nine per cent rain. That is, a mix of H_2O plus various trace elements of oxides and pollutants. But there's one particulate per billion that I haven't been able to trace. Something highly unusual that is, perhaps, a secret ingredient,' he mused, thinking back to Kenneth's show-and-tell all those years ago.

So we have rain with a secret ingredient, nodded Lara.

'And as for the soup . . .' Professor Cortex wandered over to a green plant perched on top of his cluttered desk and snapped off a stalk. 'My tests show that this chicken soup contains a little additional flavouring.' He paused. 'But this, we do know, is a herb. Thyme to be specific.'

Lara didn't get it. *What's the big deal about a little soup flavouring?* She cooked a mean Thai green curry and that contained all sorts of different herbs and spices. The professor was already a step ahead, however, and placed a hefty, dusty encyclopaedia in front of her with a thud.

'Page two hundred and forty-one,' he indicated with a flourish.

Lara leafed through the weighty tome and arrived at the correct page. Her eyesight not being quite as good as it was, she extended her arms a little to help focus the tiny print. *Thyme is a herb used to flavour cooking dishes . . . I know all this.* Then she saw it: *Down thyme: a particularly rare form of the variety that can cause sadness, unhappiness and mood swings . . .*

'What's more, GM451, down thyme has addictive properties. If you eat one bowl of soup, you will feel depressed. But you'll immediately want more soup. In fact, you'll *need* it.'

Lara looked up at the professor. *Kenneth Soop is deliberately trying to make the town feel miserable! And when they turn to the remedy – good old chicken soup – they get addicted?* She shook her head in disbelief, picked up a pencil in her paw and scribbled: *But why would he do such a thing?*

The professor pointed to a framed black and white picture on his desk. Lara looked at the cute white-coated boy with the wonky spectacles and cheesy grin. He seemed very cheery compared to the gaunt boy who stood next to him. The taller boy was holding a metal dish with an antenna.

'That's a younger me and a younger Kenneth Soop with Mr Dewitt our old head teacher. Liked egg . . . from what I remember.' He paused while Lara compared the photo of a slightly podgy small professor to the slightly podgy big professor, stifling a doggie laugh and attempting to disguise it as a cough. 'It really is no laughing matter, GM451,' he said sternly. 'Kenneth was different, but not in a good way. He wasn't normal. He wasn't like the rest of us . . .'

Lara stifled another canine snigger. *You, Prof? Normal?*

'That contraption he's holding is the Climacto-sphere 1960. A cloud-making device. Kenneth is the man we're looking for. The trouble is, we can't seem to find him. All this cloud has made it impossible for our spy satellites to locate him. And that, GM451, is where you come in . . .' Professor Cortex opened the palm of his hand to reveal a small silver disc with a hole in. 'Your new "smart" dog tag: soon to be standard issue for all our animal agents. It contains a minuscule transmitter that will track wherever you go and hopefully lead us to Soop.' The professor flipped the 'smart' tag as if he were tossing a coin. 'Heads or tails?' he grinned.

Lara watched the coin spin through the air. *I don't mind head or tails*, she thought. *If the mission is to catch a baddie, I'm feeling lucky!*

7. *Shady Dealings*

Ken Soop was unhappy; he wasn't happy unless he was unhappy. For as long as he could remember, he'd always preferred to be miserable. Laughing, joking and smiling tended to make him feel nauseous. In fact, you could say that happiness made him feel sick.

Finally he'd found a way of ridding the world of sunshine; life was far better under a dark cloud. Everyone was starting to see things his way – his glass wasn't just half empty, it was bone dry. Of course, when the time was right he'd bring a little sunshine back into people's lives. That's if the price was right . . .

Mr Dewitt shuffled across the floor and pulled the lever. With his 'egg-spert' know-how, the chickens were producing more snot than ever. The glass dome retracted. Soop plunged the large red button, activating the Cloud Maker once more. Streaks of black lightning shot into the already darkened sky, adding to the vast black cloud overhead. The smell of burnt chicken slime filled the warehouse; it would soon be raining down all over town, further adding to people's unhappiness.

Outside in the courtyard, another truck was loaded, ready to deliver the next consignment of Ken Soop's Chicken Soup. Demand was rising hourly, exactly according to Soop's plan. The giant Great Danes were clambering behind the tinted windows of the cab, getting ready to accompany their master on his mission to spread the bad news even further.

Soop placed a long, skinny forefinger up his right nostril and rummaged around. His finger withdrew with something green and glistening on the end. After close examination, Ken Soop carefully relocated it, this time to his left ear-hole. A chicken sneezed. *Pointless, flightless creatures. They should be grateful I'm putting them to good use . . .*

Back in the professor's secret lab, the elevator dropped like a stone. Lara and the professor were rapidly making their way even further under-ground, from 'top secret' to 'bottom secret'. The prof's eyes were dancing. He had a brilliant mind, and enjoyed demonstrating the 'edge' he hoped his inventions would give the agents. From experience, Lara knew that his gadgets didn't always have the desired effect, but they'd saved her life on more than one occasion. A funny feeling in her tummy signalled that the elevator had come to an abrupt halt.

They exited the lift into a bright, white laboratory containing an assortment of objects, some looking rather mundane and others far less ordinary. Resting on top of a mannequin positioned in the corner was a rainbow-coloured woolly hat. The professor placed it on his smooth, bald head and grinned at Lara. Lara tipped her head to one side. *Err . . . Very nice, Prof. But where's the spy gear?* The professor continued, undeterred by Lara's expression.

'They say that every dark cloud has a silver lining, GM451 – and this is it!' Professor Cortex removed the beanie and turned it inside-out to reveal a shiny, reflective material. 'That cloud brings bad news. Spend too long underneath it and you become soaked – literally saturated in sad thoughts. The inside of this hat is made from pure, woven sunbeams, condensed to provide a protective layer. Collecting sunbeams is a tricky business, GM451. And weaving them even trickier. It's their wavelengths, you see. They arrive as long waves but rebound off the earth much shorter. Catching them as they come in is the key . . .' He looked at Lara's glazed eyes. 'You don't need to know the ins and outs. In short, it'll make sure you stay thinking clearly – whatever the weather.'

Lara wasn't so convinced. She pulled it over her ears and checked out her reflection in the full-size mirror. The ear that always stuck up stayed true to form and popped out. Lara grimaced. *I'm supposed to be the world's Number-one Spy Dog! Blending in to my surroundings? I'm not sure this will help me to stay 'undercover'.*

Undeterred, the professor moved on to his next invention – which Lara noticed looked a lot like her bike.

'An exact replica of your bicycle,' he continued, 'except for one small detail.'

The prof straddled the red BMX and began weaving around the room erratically, struggling to pedal while remaining sat on the seat. Lara barked and mimicked standing while holding imaginary handlebars. *Try standing up, Professor; it's much easier.*

The professor did as Lara had instructed, and no longer looked quite so wobbly. Just as the Spy Dog thought she was going to have to run alongside him like she did when teaching Ollie how to ride, Professor Cortex pulled a wheelie before taking off from the ground altogether. He circled the room a couple of times, before gradually stopping pedalling and returning to the floor with a gentle squeeze of the rear brake. *WOW! Now that's more like it . . .*

'I'm rather proud of this one, GM451,' the professor enthused. 'The air in the tyres has been replaced by hyper-compressed helium; squeeze the end of the handlebars for a dose of "big air"!'

Lara was grinning from ear to ear. *Wait till Ollie sees this!*

Back at the Cooks' house, Ben looked like he needed some cheering up. After falling out with his sister, they were only communicating by text. That is, until he ran out of credit. Ben lay back on his bed and looked at the ceiling. The rain carried on hammering against his window. Sophie was sat playing on the rug in her room. Ollie was trying his best to amuse himself. He was currently scaling an imaginary rock face after first wading through a rushing river in order to escape from a gang of cowboys in hot pursuit. His bedroom certainly looked wild.

Mum and Dad sat in the lounge, channel hopping. The children could hear Dad grumbling about the 'stupid weather man, always getting it wrong' and 'How could the whole of Britain be enjoying its best summer in fifty years, except this town?'

The front door opened, and Spud and Star returned empty-handed. After they'd explained what had happened in the supermarket, no one felt in the mood for chicken soup any more.

The dark cloud hanging over the town seemed to be getting bigger – and darker. Even the rain seemed to be getting wetter.

Professor Cortex clearly thought that he'd saved the best of his gadgets until last.

'It's often the simple ideas that work best,' he chirped.

Lara wasn't so sure. She stared at her reflection in the mirror. She wasn't convinced by the rainbow beanie, but the professor's 'extendable sticky lead' was perhaps a step too far.

'I've even sold the idea to NASA,' the professor explained. 'You know, for spacewalks and suchlike. The technology is based on fly's feet. And aphids. Although the effect is more "Spiderman". This doggie lead is made of a special stretchy substance – I'll spare you the details, GM451 – with sticky stuff on the end. So it stretches *and* sticks.'

Lara's raised eyebrows indicated that she was struggling to keep up, so the professor tried again.

'Have you noticed that flies can walk on windows? That's because they have special hairy feet. Well, I say "hairy", they're actually cilia. Microscopic protrusions. Here's one, magnified of course,' he gabbled, sweeping his hand towards a PowerPoint slide that was beamed on to the wall.

Lara nodded encouragingly.

'That's my girl, GM451. I used the idea to create synthetic fibres that exactly match their cilia. The result? See this doggie lead?' The professor took the lead and swung it like a lasso, before letting go of one end. The lead stretched as far as the far wall, where the other end stuck. The white-coated scientist beamed. He pulled hard. 'Fixed tight. Genius or what, GM451? Imagine swinging around like that Spider chappie! Whoosh, whoosh,' he enthused, waving his arms like a maniac.

Lara took the end of the stretchy lead and gave it a firm tug. *I'm a dog, not a spider*, she thought. *I can't really see a need. But even 'retired' Spy Dogs should always be prepared!*

The toilet elevator came to a halt with a gentle *ping*. Lara found herself staring at the inside of the portable loo once more. She reached for the door handle and paused, her mind registering the 'engaged' sign. She was to find one of Soop's delivery lorries and follow it – wherever it went.

My mission is simple. Find him and stop him.

She pawed her new 'smart' tag. The professor had assured her that help would be close at hand.

8. The Delivery

Dad was singing in the shower again. He couldn't get the new chicken-soup jingle out of his head. *'Soop's soup. Picks you up when you're feeling down . . .'*

Mum was standing at the door, yelling at him to stop.

'Put a sock in it! It's depressing enough with this awful weather,' she said, banging on the door. 'Your singing's so bad, I think you might be causing it.'

The Cook household was not a happy place.

Thunder rumbled across the sky. Ken Soop stood outside his chicken empire, rocking back and forth on his heels, arms clasped behind his back. Soop was thinking. The Cloud Maker was working better than he had hoped. There were miserable people all over town. People feeling down were flocking to the supermarkets looking for something to pick them up, to make them feel better. Tins of Ken Soop's Chicken Soup were flying off the shelves.

His master plan was to create clouds over the next town and the next town, until the whole country was depressed. But there was a problem: sales were soaring and he was running out of chicken stock. The old man had already doubled the amount of pepper in the chicken's feed, but even with the extra sneezing they weren't producing enough. No: he needed to make more soup and he needed to keep the rain falling. He needed more chickens and he hoped Mr Dewitt could 'Dewitt'.

The ancient man's white hair blew wildly in the wind. Young Kenneth was relying on him and he wasn't about to let him down. No one knew more about chickens than he did. The farm sheepdogs had put up a brave fight but the sheer size of Mr Heinz and Mr Campbell meant it was no contest. Two hundred and thirty-five hens were secured in the back of the wagon. The old man couldn't remember the address of

Kenneth's factory so it had been written down for him. His frail hands gripped the steering wheel and he leant forward into a driving position, his faltering eyes squinting through the windscreen. The lorry eased away. It was only thirty miles to the factory, but at twenty-three miles per hour it was a long haul.

The last of the trolleys had been unloaded from the back of the truck. The pimply teenager stopped for a minute and rubbed the base of his aching back. He looked up at the tinted windows of the cab and wondered about its occupant.

Most of the delivery drivers would at least acknowledge you, some would even give you a hand. Ken Soop's lorries were different. They just drove in and parked while you emptied the trailer, before driving off again. Most unfriendly. Not a word, or even a wave. The

boy shrugged and turned to make his way back into the store.

Ken Soop turned the ignition and the truck rumbled into life like a dragon awakening. His spidery fingers turned the steering wheel as the vast transporter exited the loading bay. A spindle of snot seeped from his nose almost in slow motion. As he pulled out on to the main road, the other cars kept a wary distance, not wanting to argue with a forty-ton truck. Soop was bigger than every other vehicle on the road. He also considered himself better. He was in charge. He was in control. And he intended to make sure people knew it. The dastardly man decided to have some fun on his return journey.

On the hill overlooking the loading bay, Lara snapped the chinstrap of her helmet before kicking off and careering down the slope. She needed to keep close, but not too close; it was important that Soop didn't know he was being followed and try to escape. *And then we'll see about cheering things up a bit,* thought Lara, wiping the rain from her eyes with the back of her paw.

The lorry was gathering speed down the main high street, and had just shot straight through a red light, narrowly avoiding a mobility scooter.

Whoa! This guy's not going to stop for anyone! I need to slow him down a little.

Lara peddled furiously, taking a short cut across the park and using the see-saw as a handy ramp to hurdle the fence before rejoining the main road.

Ken Soop put his foot down, the lorry accelerating around a corner, tyres squealing. The evil man howled in delight and turned on the radio; heavy metal – power felt good! Weaving from side to side, he sent a wheelie bin flying and splashed a cyclist.

Lara needed to think fast and pedal even faster. *If I don't do something to put the brakes on, then someone's going to get seriously hurt. But if I stop him completely then there's no chance of finding out whoever's behind this whole miserable business* . . . She felt helpless to know what to do. *Almost a little deflated* . . . *Hmmm* . . .

Lara had to carry out her plan before the lorry had left town, otherwise it would be too late. She was only going to get one shot at this. The truck turned right and Lara turned left, pedalling for all she was worth. While she couldn't match the lorry for speed, she knew all the short cuts.

Lara was starting to puff hard, and the wind was whistling through the hole in her ear. *Phew . . . I'm not sure how much longer I can keep this up. Maybe I should just face it – I'm getting too old for all this. Maybe my Spy Dog days are over. I'm a has-been! Wait a minute . . .*

Lara slammed on the brakes and the BMX screeched to a halt. She stared into space, the wind and rain driving into her eyes. She blinked and shook her head, wondering if she had really been considering giving up. The rain carried on pouring down, soaking her fur through and through. She looked at the ever-present black cloud looming above the town. *Has-been . . . been . . . beanie. That's it! The rain is making me feel miserable! I need the professor's woolly hat!*

Lara quickly rummaged in the pocket under her saddle and pulled out the rainbow-coloured beanie. *No time to remove my bike helmet.* She pulled it over the top of her cycle hat, giving her something of a 'rasta-dog' appearance. Smiling once more, Lara set off, determined to slow the lorry down. The storm cloud had made her feel down – but she certainly wasn't out!

On the edge of town was a long straight road, which Lara knew the lorry would have to take; the only alternative would mean taking a road over a small humpback bridge and that would risk getting the lorry stuck. After a couple more bends and several hairy cross-country detours, Lara saw that her hunch had been right. The truck was at the other end of the road, heading straight in her direction. *Good; there's no other traffic on the road – at least no one else is in any danger.*

In the distance, Ken Soop spotted a scruffy-looking patchwork mongrel, parked up on a bike in the middle of the road. He frowned; a mutt on a bike was odd enough. But it appeared to be wearing some sort of . . . tea cosy. No matter – he pressed his boot flat to the floor, the truck gathering speed. The mutt would soon be dust. Lara stared at the approaching truck, unflinching, before racing directly towards it. Soop's eyes widened, unsure what to make of it all. Of course, in this game of chicken there was only going to be one winner. He wiped the back of his hand across his dribbly nose and hunched over the wheel as the gap closed.

Lara was concentrating. She had to get this

right – or else. The gap grew less and less, neither bike nor truck deviating from the collision course. Lara braced herself; this lady was not for turning.

Soop started to sweat, a bead of perspiration forming on his brow. He adjusted his grip on the steering wheel. The bike was getting closer and closer now; he could see the whites of Lara's eyes. At the point of impact Soop shut his eyes and flinched, waiting to hear the crunch.

9. Under Pressure

Lara had waited until the last possible moment before squeezing the handlebars. The helium exploded into her tyres, giving her instant 'big air'. She missed the onrushing truck by milli-metres, her rear wheel brushing the roof of the cab. Lara pulled her left brake sharply, landing skilfully on the roof of the trailer, her rear wheel skidding around in a one hundred and eighty degree arc to face the direction in which they were travelling.

Phew – that was close!

She gathered herself for a moment, her heart thumping loudly in her chest.

Soop opened his eyes, a little embarrassed that he'd closed them in the first place. The dog had seemingly vanished into thin air. It was nowhere to be seen. Soop shook his head and looked at the clock on the dashboard. He wondered if he'd been on the road for too long and was starting to imagine things. He assumed the dog would be squashed, a black and white rug in the middle of the road.

Meanwhile, Lara had attached one end of her sticky dog lead to the roof of the trailer and expertly abseiled down to dangle over the wheel arches.

Using the titanium clasp from her dog collar, she severed the valve and gently released some of the air from the huge tyres. *Not too much now . . . just enough to slow this thing down to a safe speed.* She hoped that Soop wouldn't spot her in the side mirrors. With a snap of her wrist, the lead retracted to return her to the roof. *Now for the other side . . .*

Lara descended the opposite side of the truck in one perfectly judged leap, positioning herself next to the barrelling wheels. *Steady does it, just need to let a little air out.* All of a sudden, Lara's dangling silhouette was illuminated by the dazzling headlights of an onrushing truck coming from the opposite direction. *Cat litter! If I don't do something fast, I'm dog meat!*

Planting her feet on the edge of the wheel rim, Lara bent her knees and took a deep breath. The horrified oncoming driver spotted her and pulled his horn, blaring a loud warning.

Focus, Lara. Clear your mind.

She closed her eyes for a brief second, meditating and drawing inner strength.

Just as the lorry was almost upon her, Lara snapped open her eyes and pushed off from the side of the trailer. She sailed over the top of the truck just in time, narrowly avoiding a messy collision, before swinging back to resume her position by the wheel arch. *Phew! That was close!* Lara let out a sigh of relief, before letting out a little more air from the tyres. She could sense that the truck was already slowing down, and the journey might be a little safer from now on. Another flick of the wrist and Lara's lead retracted her to the relative safety of the top of the lorry.

Now it's just a case of sitting tight and waiting.

As Lara and the truck disappeared over the horizon, her silver 'smart' tag rolled to a halt at the side of the road. Broken off in all the commotion, the tracking device was tracking no more. Although she didn't know it yet, GM451 was on her own.

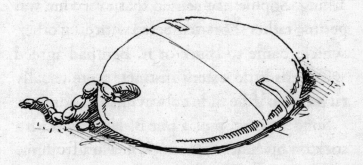

Ben, Sophie, Ollie and the pups had called an emergency meeting. It just so happened to be in the laundry room. Ben had suggested they meet there because the sound of the rumbling washing machine would mean they couldn't be overheard. It wasn't that they liked keeping secrets from Mum and Dad, just that they didn't want them to worry. Parents are very good at worrying.

Lara had been gone for some time and there had been no news from her. That wasn't unusual, but everyone couldn't help feeling she could probably use a helping hand. She was supposed to be 'semi-retired' after all, a fact that she kept conveniently forgetting.

The dark cloud had been spreading its misery over the town and the rain still hadn't stopped falling. Sophie had sensed that everyone was getting rather short-tempered with each other, which, come to think of it, Ben had agreed with. His little sister's instincts were usually right, even if he didn't always like to admit it.

Spud sat on top of a pile of laundry with a sock on his head. Star shook her head at him.

'This is no time for mucking about, bro,' she frowned. 'We need to work out how to help Mum!'

'No problem, sis – I'll put a sock in it!' Spud giggled.

Ollie started giggling too. He loved it when Spud clowned around.

'Maybe we should try contacting Professor Cortex?' Ben ventured. 'He might be able to tell us something – or at least stop us from worrying.'

Sophie and Star exchanged glances with each other. This had the feel of another adventure, and that wasn't always a good thing . . .

10. Dirty Washing

It was night-time when Mr Soop finally drew the truck up to the large iron gates leading to his ~~chicken~~ empire. The compound was situated in the middle of a disused industrial estate. It seemed eerily quiet – apart from what Lara thought sounded strangely like an occasional 'cluck'. She absently placed her paw on her 'smart' tag – only to discover it was no longer there! Lara's head dropped. The rules of this game seemed to be changing fast. It was now down to her alone to stop Soop.

The gates appeared to open automatically, allowing the truck through to park in the courtyard. Kenneth Soop climbed down from his cab and slammed the door shut behind him. He stretched, his bottom erupting, a roast-chicken aroma making Lara's eyes bulge. The man made his way over to one of the warehouses, where he vanished through a small side door. Lara stayed put for a moment, wafting her paw across her nose, looking around to see if it was safe to investigate. After a moment, a huge Great Dane appeared, patrolling by the perimeter fence. Lara's eyes were drawn to a sign: DANGER! TRESPASSERS WILL BE BITTEN.

Visitors are obviously not welcome.

She waited until he had disappeared down the side of one of the warehouses, before skilfully freewheeling her bike across the front of the truck and landing on the ground via the top of a wheelie bin.

Gazing around in the darkness, Lara spied a glass dome on one of the warehouse roofs. Lights reflected in the glass signalled some sort of activity down below.

Looks like a good place to start. Let's see what they're so keen on protecting . . .

Lara dumped her bike in the bushes and set off on four paws, aiming in the direction of the metal fire escape that zigzagged its way up the side of the building.

A patrolling Great Dane suddenly re-emerged from the side of a building. Lara froze. *He's huge!*

She couldn't recall Great Danes being particularly fierce but she knew dogs ended up being like their owners. *So if he has a fierce owner?* Lara shrank into the shadows. The Great Dane sniffed the air, his ears pricked. Lara watched, controlling her breathing and hoping her pounding heart wasn't as loud as it felt. The huge animal put his nose to the floor and sniffed. He followed the scent to Lara's abandoned bike and sounded the alert. His bark was as loud as his bite. 'Woof woof, intruder alert,' he began.

Lara only had a split second to decide what to do. *I could hide? But with his sense of smell, my chances aren't great. And if he barks again it will attract people. Probably with guns.*

It was a no-brainer. The retired Spy Dog filled her lungs with oxygen and leapt from the bushes. The black and white blur spiralled in mid-air. She had recently been watching martial-arts movies on Ben's iPad and was, on reflection, a little too enthusiastic in her attack. She let out a piercing wolf-like howl and aimed for the Great Dane's huge legs. She missed, landing squarely on his back, and was now hanging on like a skinny cowboy on the back of a huge bucking bronco. *Yeee-haaa!*

Mr Heinz was under attack. He barked louder and leapt around, trying to rid himself of his furry passenger.

Lara fell to the dirt. *Ooof! That's a long way down.* She received a kick to her nose and a stamp to her tail. She stood groggily and raised her aching head to face a dog that was at least three times her size. *I can take him*, she thought. *But* w*hy's he grinning?*

Lara's theory about 'dogs being like their owners' was true. Pure evil stood behind her. Soop swung the baseball bat and Lara's world went dark.

The washing machine rumbled on, continuing its tumbling mantra. Star placed the dog bowl in the centre of the laundry room, before giving the rim three anti-clockwise twists. After a little flickering and crackling, a blue light stretched from bowl to ceiling. Shortly after, the rotund figure of Professor Cortex appeared, his hologram smiling broadly.

'Greetings, children, Agents Spud and Star. I trust you've received your new "smart" tags, pups?'

Ben stepped forward. 'We're hoping Lara's OK, and thought you might know where she was?'

'Ahem,' the professor coughed in the slightly guilty way he often did before admitting to knowing a little more than he'd been letting on. 'I'm sure GM451 is tickety-boo. She had been trying to track a lorry to find out where this depressing raincloud was coming from, and the disgusting chicken soup that everyone seems to be buying to make them feel better.'

The pups looked at each other.

'I knew there was something fishy going on,' woofed Star.

'Or "chickeny",' added Spud, rather lamely.

'And . . .?' added Ben.

'Err . . . I've not heard anything, as yet. I'm afraid her "smart" tag doesn't seem to be so smart . . .' The professor shuffled his feet and looked a little uncomfortable. He had hoped to have had some news by now.

'We've got to help her!' exclaimed Sophie, already fearing the worst.

'We need to find that lorry!' added Ollie, the smile having disappeared from his face.

'Is there anything else you can tell us, Professor?' asked Ben. The professor's hologram scratched its shiny head.

'The lorry had KEN SOOP'S CHICKEN SOUP written on the side. That's all we really know,' he added, almost apologetically. 'This is our man,' said the hologram, holding up a large picture of Kenneth Soop's long face. 'Oh – and lots of chickens seem to be mysteriously

vanishing in the middle of the night. Oops . . .
sorry . . . there seems to be some interference.
I'm losing the signal . . .'

With a couple of flickers and a sharp crack,
the hologram disappeared. The children and
pups looked at one another.

'How do we know where to start?' asked
Ben.

No one said anything for a minute, as they
desperately tried to come up with a plan for
helping Lara.

Sophie broke the silence, her grin lighting
up the laundry room. She beamed at Star and
Spud.

'Pups,' she said, 'I have a cunning plan.'

11. Prison

Lara's beanie had been pulled down over her eyes. Her head was pounding as she lifted a paw and revealed her left eye. *The professor's invention might stop negative thoughts, but it doesn't stop a sore head!* Her bloodshot eye caught sight of the baseball bat standing in the corner and suddenly it made sense. She had enough energy to groggily assess her prison. *A burnt-out room that smells of chicken. Black walls and soot on the floor.*

It was a struggle, but Lara raised herself and limped to the small window that was set into the door. She tried the handle. *Locked. Obviously.* The strain was almost too much but she stood tall on her hind legs and wiped the soot off the window. *Wow!*

A tall, skinny man dressed in black was inspecting a series of dials and levers attached to an assortment of containers and machines.

Kenneth Soop!

He drifted between the controls like a daddy-long-legs, administering the faintest of touches before moving on. Every now and then, Lara noticed he would to stop to unscrew a tall silver flask, taking several sips before wiping his moustache with his sleeve.

Trailing the daddy-long-legs around the warehouse were two Great Danes. Shuffling between them all was . . . *the headmaster I saw on Professor Cortex's old school photograph!* Lara's blood boiled and her head throbbed harder.

In the centre of the room was what looked like a satellite dish, pointing towards the glass sunroof. Lara's eyes weren't what they used to be and she didn't have her contact lenses in today; the rain usually played havoc with them. Spotting the various dials and read-outs, she squinted through her bloodshot eyes, trying to work out what they controlled. She didn't have to wait long to find out.

The very old man fumbled with a remote-control device, examining it closely before pulling a lever very precisely. The glass dome began to shudder and vibrate, retracting from the middle in two halves. Soop then plunged the big, red button on the control panel. Lara watched in amazement as crackling streaks of black lightning shot out of the centre of the satellite dish, filling the sky with a thick, dark smog.

Soop clapped enthusiastically. He approached Lara's window; his face so close to Lara's she could count the lumps of gristle between his rotten teeth. His voice was eerily muffled behind the triple-glazed window.

'New, improved, darker clouds,' she lip-read. 'More sadness. And more demand for my special-ingredient chicken soup,' he gloated.

Lara tried to stare him down but she wasn't sure what was more menacing, Soop or the thunder that rolled overhead.

Lara retreated to the corner of the burnt-out room and slumped down against the walls. The strain of opening her eyes was too much. Her chin rested on her paws and she sighed wearily.

This Spy Dog needs saving. In fact, the world needs saving. I hope Spud and Star are on their way.

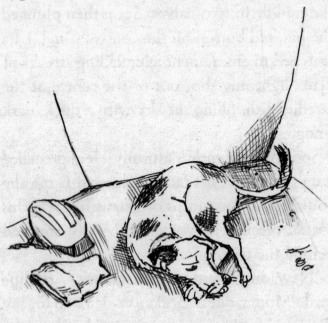

12. Winging It

Sophie had needed a minute to run the plan through her head before she dared announce it out loud. She turned from looking out of the window. 'Find Kenneth Soop and we might be able to shed some light on that pesky cloud. Find him and I bet we'll find Lara.'

Ben nodded his head in agreement. 'But how do we find him? If Lara's in trouble, we need to help her – and fast!' As the oldest of the children, he tried to stay calm so as not to worry the others, but he was feeling increasingly concerned. There was a pause, while everyone considered their next step.

'Maybe we don't have to,' suggested Sophie. 'Find him, that is. Maybe Ken Soop will come to us . . .'

Everyone turned to look at Sophie quizzically.

'Don't you see? Everything's to do with the chickens! The cloud arrives and everyone feels miserable. Sales of Ken Soop's Chicken Soup rocket. More chickens mysteriously disappear and at the same time the cloud gets bigger and bigger! Grey clouds, grey moods and grey soup. It's more than just a coincidence.'

Ben tilted his head to one side, 'But I still don't see how we're going to find Soop?'

Sophie smiled, removing a stray feather from Ollie's hair. It was time to get crafty.

Mum and Dad were somewhat bemused: pleased, but also a little puzzled. The children had been camped in Ollie's room for hours along with the twins, apparently helping to tidy up. Mum had sneaked a look not long ago, and the floor was already looking considerably tidier.

Dad looked up from his newspaper and shrugged. 'I suppose they're finally getting the message.'

Mum wasn't so sure.

'Well, I'd like to think so,' she replied, not

entirely convinced by their sudden enthusiasm for housework.

Behind the bedroom door, the carpet was certainly looking clearer. Ollie's craft set was being put to good use. Agents Spud and Star sat perfectly still on a pair of upturned crates that usually contained a wide assortment of dressing-up clothes. Ben and Sophie were just putting the finishing touches; there'd been a few alterations. Their shiny new 'smart' tags reflected each other's faces.

'How do I look?' barked Spud out of the corner of his mouth.

'Honestly?' woofed Star, her eyes resting on her brother.

'Honestly.'

'Flapping great,' she replied, deadpan.

'Oh . . . err, cool,' woofed Spud. He wasn't entirely sure if that was a good thing.

Brickfield Farm's chickens were free-range chickens. They were also the only remaining 'free' chickens for miles around, those from neighbouring farms having mysteriously disappeared over the past week. If Soop needed more chickens, then this was where he'd come to.

Even in the dead of night, the hens enjoyed stretching their legs in the fresh air, gazing at the moon and thanking their lucky stars. Life didn't get much better than this for a chicken. It was luxury living: chicken supreme.

Two particularly large chickens perched in the shadows of one of the numerous sheds, both looking a little self-conscious. One of them started to type on their mobile.

'What are you doing?' hissed Star, elbowing her brother sharply.

'Ouch!' yelped Spud. 'Playing it cool – just like you said!' he retorted.

'Chickens don't surf the internet!' Star barked with a chicken accent.

'Oh – don't they? What do they do?'

Star paused. 'Cross the road a lot? I don't know . . .'

The pups had had a makeover. They were now working undercover. Ben and Sophie's handiwork with Ollie's craft set had transformed the pups into fully fledged chicken operatives – albeit a very unusual breed. A pair of Sophie's old fairy wings had been customized with red, yellow and green feathers, disguising Star's front legs. She tried a half-hearted flap, hoping nothing fell off.

Ollie's cuddly bumblebee costume had been similarly adapted for Spud. The children had needed to source some extra feathers from one of the pillows out of the spare room, but the overall effect seemed to work OK. Each dog sported one of Ben's brightly coloured pair of goalie gloves on the top of their head. Half a chocolate-orange wrapper moulded around the dogs' noses completed the look.

The other chickens continued to go blissfully

about their business, pecking the ground and clucking. Occasionally one would strut over to take a closer look at the pups, before shrugging and resuming their search for scattered feed. The rain started again, the ever-present cloud giving no let-up from the miserable weather. Star shivered, and hugged her wings a little tighter. She looked down the road, but there was still no sign; she kept her wings crossed that this was going to work.

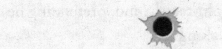

13. Spy-jacked

Mr Dewitt trundled the lorry along the outskirts of Brickfield, the only vehicle on the road at that late hour. His wipers smeared the windscreen, as they had done last night and the night before that. Classical music blared out of the stereo.

The 'runaway pensioner' had been given the job of finding more chickens to keep up with the demand for soup. The headmaster knew about chickens – children and chickens. They both required direction and firm discipline. On the top of the hill was a free-range farm, where the chickens pretty much wandered about doing as they pleased. Mr Dewitt thought it would be a doddle; open up the back of the truck and simply bung the birds in the trailer: job done.

Star spotted the dull headlights meandering up the hill and nudged her brother.

'Eh, what?' spluttered Spud, pretending he'd been awake all along.

'We've got company,' woofed Star, nodding in the direction of the approaching truck. Ollie and Sophie's hunch had been right. Chickens had been mysteriously going missing all over town every night for a week now – everywhere, that is, apart from Brickfield Farm. Tonight it was their turn.

'What do we do?' hissed Spud.

'Run around like headless chickens – I think,' barked Star. Which was exactly what the rest of the brood were doing. Panic had set in among the farm's residents, unsettled by this sudden, unexpected visit. Chickens raced around in every direction, colliding with each other and generally getting into a flap. Star was tempted to tell them all to calm down but resisted, recognizing that a little fuss might help distract attention from them.

Mr Dewitt brought the lorry to a halt, switched off the engine and eased his creaking body down from the cab. He was very tired but all he needed to do was chuck the chicks in the back. He shuddered at the thought of the retirement home.

Mr Heinz and Mr Campbell jumped down and got to work. The stupid birds were milling around everywhere, tripping over each other and apologizing repeatedly.

'Shhhhh! This is our chance,' cluck-woofed Spud, realizing that Mr Dewitt's back was turned. 'Careful of those huge dogs!'

He grabbed his sister by the paw and they joined the crowd of chickens.

'Keep your head down,' warned Star. 'These disguises were the best we could do, but they won't stand up to close scrutiny. And those dogs have a keen sense of smell. However good the disguises are, we don't smell like birds!'

The tailgate had been lowered and hens were being herded aboard, single file. Mr Dewitt was at the bottom of the gangplank, flexing his cane, counting them in. 'Ninety-seven . . . ninety-eight . . .' He always was good with numbers.

Spud and Star shuffled forward, nervously awaiting their turn. Star's heart was hammering inside her chest. 'Ninety-nine,' counted the old man as the puppy hopped by.

It was Spud's turn. His large belly meant he was the biggest chicken by far. He hopped on to the gangplank, overacting terribly. His sister heard him attempt a cluck.

For goodness' sake, bro, she thought. *There's no need!* She cast her eye behind and watched her bother attempt to flap his wings. His left wing fell off. *Oops!*

'Hold it right there,' shouted the old man. He approached the chicken-pup. Spud decided not to attempt another cluck. He hopped one more time and pecked at the plank with his fake beak.

It was dark and rainy, so the man came in for a closer look. He bent over until his nose was level with Spud, squinting at the pup before unfurling a piece of paper.

'Kenneth said one hundred,' he muttered. 'So you, big fatty, are the last one.'

A relieved Spud fell into the back of the truck with ninety-eight hens and one other puppy.

The back door was slammed and locked.

'Big fatty?' laughed his sister.

Spud snorted. He wasn't cut out to be a chicken.

14. Chicken Run

Ken Soop was ecstatically unhappy. Everything had gone according to plan. The town was turning utterly miserable. People expected the worst and he delivered the worst. He, Ken Soop, was finally in control. Sadness ruled and Mr Dewitt had been right all along; it was only the winning that mattered. It felt so good! He wondered what people would pay for a dose of sunshine. *One million? Seaside resorts would pay a lot more. Maybe I can sell sunny days as 'buy one get one free'?* he considered.

A droplet of snot teetered on the end of his whistling ski-jump nose, before being wiped away with the back of his sleeve. The silvery trail glistened for a moment before soaking in. Unscrewing the cap of his flask, Soop drank deeply, eyes closed, savouring the special ingredients. Several sticky lumps snared in his moustache; something for later.

Ken Soop paraded down the endless rows of birds, congratulating himself for being so clever; it took a genius to create such misery. And soon he'd be in a position to put the final phase of his master plan into action. When the constant black clouds were so depressing that everyone had had enough, he would sell 'sunny days'. *An auction*, he decided. *A sunny day for the highest bidder. Priceless!*

It was after midnight. The children were hoping that Mum and Dad would be sound asleep as they rose from their beds and padded downstairs. Sophie quietly closed the door to the laundry room. Ben gave the rim of the dog-bowl three anti-clockwise twists and stepped back. It wasn't long before Professor Cortex's hologram crackled into view again.

'We're wondering if you've heard anything?' hissed Sophie.

They were all desperate for news of the dogs.

Professor Cortex frowned. 'My orbiting spy satellites have tracked the micro-chips hidden inside Agents Star and Spud's collars. I believe they are due to arrive at the suspect's destination any second.' Professor Cortex looked serious for a moment as he looked down. 'Ah yes, I can see. If they maintain their current course, the pups are heading for an old disused warehouse high in the hills. The next few hours will be crucial.'

'Yes, but – have you heard from Lara?' ventured Ben, not really wanting to ask.

Professor Cortex hesitated. 'GM451's signal has gone dead. We're hoping that she's still in one piece . . .' The professor looked down at his feet and the children turned to each other, none of them daring to say what was on their minds. 'I'm in my van right now. I'm going to Soop's factory to confront him. He needs to be stopped.'

'We want to come too,' demanded Ollie.

The professor's hologram scratched its head, looking as worried as a hologram could. He knew this was a dangerous mission and he knew that Mrs Cook wouldn't take kindly to them coming along. The hologram was quiet for an awfully long time.

'Professor Cortex, can you hear us?' demanded Sophie. 'We want to come too.'

The hologram vanished with a pop. Ben smashed one fist into the other in frustration.

'He did that deliberately! He doesn't want us to come. He doesn't want to put us in danger.'

The children jumped as there was a soft tapping at the laundry-room window. Ollie looked terrified, hiding in a pile of dirty laundry.

The tapping came again, this time with a muffled hiss. '*Pssst.*'

Ben edged towards the window and swung it open. The professor's bald head popped into view.

'I was transmitting the hologram from my van, parked outside your house.' Professor Cortex sighed, 'I might live to regret this, but I know how much you love GM451.' He stretched his arm in and helped Ben out first. Then Sophie and Ollie. 'Come on, gang. We've got an egg-venture to crack.' The kids couldn't help but smile at the prof's gag: it was a joke how unfunny it was!

Mr Dewitt reversed the lorry up against the large warehouse doors; not a moment too soon for Spud and Star. They'd spent the last two hours cooped up inside the trailer with a bunch of hysterical chickens. Star had tried to suggest controlled breathing techniques to calm them, but to no avail. The chickens were in a considerable flap.

Star looked at her brother, 'Remember – act chicken.'

Spud nodded, 'Woof. I mean – cluck.' He checked his goalie glove was still positioned on top of his head. It was drooping but still in place. His one remaining wing hung limply at his side.

The bolt slipped with a clunk before the back

of the trailer opened and torchlight streamed in. A great deal of loud barking ensued, as Mr Campbell and Mr Heinz set about ushering the chickens down the ramp and into the warehouse. Feathers flew everywhere, as birds trampled over each other in an attempt to keep away from the growling Great Danes.

Star hurried past them. Spud made sure he kept the side with his wing towards the dogs. The pups and chickens were noisily herded into a row of steel pens. It had been a long night and the chickens were hungry. Some of the new arrivals were already pecking at the specially prepared feed and sneezing; they just couldn't help themselves. It wouldn't be long before they were fuelling the Cloud Maker, creating an atmosphere of grumpiness that would send customers all over the country rushing for their comforting chicken soup.

15. 'Whooooof'

Spud tried to keep his head down as he was ushered into the warehouse. He woofed a few 'clucks', in an attempt to make himself sound like a real chicken, and just hoped that his disguise did the trick. Neither of the large dogs currently barking instructions at them seemed to suspect anything. *So far, so good . . .*

Star followed a little way behind her brother and was also keeping low. She concentrated on flapping her 'wings', and bobbing her head, even pretending to peck at the floor a couple of times.

Mr Heinz had taken up his position on top of an old wooden crate overlooking proceedings. He watched as the new arrivals were channelled into their pens, before being positioned in front of the peppery feed. He rubbed his eyes with a large paw and blinked. Something didn't feel quite right. Or maybe something didn't look quite right. He cast his eyes along the rows and rows of chickens that were being secured: left, right and then back again. For some reason, his gaze rested upon one particular chicken. This one looked somehow different from the rest. It was slightly larger, and . . . Mr Heinz couldn't quite put his paw on it.

He jumped down from the crate and went over to inspect this particular chicken a little more closely. He reached the end of the row and stood peering at the chicken.

'Cluck,' said Spud, and then, 'cluck,' again. He gave a flap of his remaining wing for good measure. Mr Heinz was far from convinced. He looked around at the other chickens. They all had beady red chicken eyes. *And yet this extra-large bird has big brown doggie eyes?* He reached out his paw and touched the chocolate-orange wrapper disguising Spud's black nose, which subsequently fell off.

'Err, good evening,' woofed Spud innocently. 'Cluck cluck?' he said hopefully.

The Great Dane's eyes grew wide in horror as he realized that this was no chicken. He opened his mouth to shout for help, 'HEY!

Ummphhhh . . .' Star had leapt from her perch
and silenced the Great Dane with a swift chop
to the top of his head. *Not so 'great' now!*

Dazed, the huge animal slumped to the floor.
'Thanks, sis,' wagged Spud, shaking off
the rest of his costume. 'OK, spread out. We
need to find Mum – and fast.' The two pups
scampered along the rows and rows of chickens, checking the pens as they went.

Spud let himself out into the yard, sniffing
hard. *Mum's bike*, he thought, his nose taking

him to the bushes. He unclipped the saddlebag and peered inside, snaffling the 'extendable lead'. He returned to show his sister. Star had also made a discovery. She beckoned her brother and pushed a door ajar. The Spy Pups peered into the next room.

'Bingo!'

The pups gazed in awe at the sheer scale of the machine. Kenneth Soop was rocking back and forth on his heels, a sense of contentment on his face. All of a sudden, the door burst open and in rushed Professor Cortex and the children.

'Not good,' woofed Star.

'Affirmative, sis,' agreed her brother. '*Very* not good!'

'The game's up, Soop,' yelled the professor. 'We know your evil plan and we have you surrounded,' he continued, in an unconvincing double-fib.

'Maximus?' Soop purred, recognizing the white coat and sticking-plaster spectacles. 'Maximus Cortex? Why, it must be nearly sixty years!'

'You'll be getting at least sixty years for this, you evil baddie,' added Ollie for good measure. 'And where's our dog?'

'Your dog?' Soop repeated. 'That black and white mongrel is *your* dog? This dog?' he smirked, walking to the blackened window and pointing at Lara's startled face. Her paw was tapping frantically on the window, her frenzied barking muffled behind three layers of glass.

'Noooo, kids! Get out. Escape while you can!'

The family pet was way ahead of the game. Her head was still hurting but it hadn't stopped her working out the entire plan, including where she was imprisoned.

The puppies watched in horror as Kenneth Soop flicked a lever marked 'ignite'.

There was an ominous rumbling and a large *whoosh* that nobody could place except Lara. She shrank back from the flames as the giant oven ignited.

'Your dog has trespassed on to my property. Into my giant chicken oven to be exact,' he snarled. 'Tonight there will be a change of menu. Apologies, customers, but the chicken soup is off. Today's special . . . is *hot dog*.'

16. Hot Dog

Mr Soop stood calmly with his tentacle-like fingers clasped behind his back, rocking gently back on his heels, eagerly anticipating the children's horror. He'd summoned Mr Heinz and Mr Campbell, and although only one dog had appeared, a growling Great Dane was enough to dissuade Ben from running at the man and pummelling him with his fists.

Sophie was sobbing. 'It's an oven. Poor Lara. He's cooking poor Lara.'

'You're a big bully,' shouted Ollie, his bottom lip trembling. 'And anyway, she's not an ordinary dog, she's a Spy Dog. So you and that Great Dame don't stand a chance.'

'Dane,' corrected Soop, emphasizing the 'n'.

'And him as well,' agreed Ollie.

'It does seem a little, you know, harsh?'

suggested Professor Cortex, sliding his spectacles back up to the top of his nose. 'I mean, Kenneth, there must be a way to sort this rumpus out. You're a reasonable chap. Surely we can laugh the whole thing off and just call it a misunderstanding?'

'Oh, there's no *misunderstanding*, Maximus. Remember, it's not the taking part that counts.' He eyed the assembled crowd and his voice fell to an eerie sneer. 'It's the winning. And we both know that there can only be one winner.'

Lara was by now getting more than a little hot under the collar. She looked around frantically for some way out of the oven, desperately trying to shield the heat with her paws. *Think, Lara, think!* Her brain frantically flicked through her science lessons with the professor. *Thermo-dynamics. Heat. Flames. Hot air. Hot air rises! There must be a chimney!*

She looked up and, sure enough, at the far side of the huge oven was a blackened chimney. Spurred on by a glimmer of hope, Lara sprinted across for a closer look. She banged a paw on the blackened wall and the soot fell away. *A ladder*, she gasped. *Built into the oven wall. Presumably an escape route in case anyone, or anything, gets trapped in here.* She saw that it disappeared up the chimney. *Hooray!*

The hot dog knew she was only going to get one shot at this. The temperature was rising and her body felt weaker by the minute. The flames were licking at the oven walls and she noticed a temperature gauge with the needle in the red zone. Her tongue lolloped as she gasped for breath. *I hate ladders*, she thought. *These paws are rubbish for climbing.*

She took a run up at the ladder and launched herself upwards, paws scrabbling and teeth biting down on rung number four. *I wish I were a cat*, she slobbered, choking on soot but not letting go of the rung. Her back legs got a foothold and she leapt again.

Rung six. She gripped her teeth into the ladder and hooked her paws around the rungs.

The retired Spy Dog knew this was life or death. The heat was rising and so was she. Lara just hoped she could make it in time.

'NOW,' woofed Star as she darted from her hiding place. What Star lacked in size, she made up for in speed. It was her job to go for the legs. The Great Dane's eyes were fixed on the children and he only spied the black and white blur at the last moment – too late to stop her rugby-tackling his front legs. As the huge dog fell on to his front knees, Spud swung from nowhere, Spider-pup-style, and took his hindquarters. What Spud lacked in speed, he made up for in bulk. The Great Dane yelped in pain and fear as the dead-leg forced him on to his back knees too. In an instant, Star had used the Spider-lead to tie the huge dog's legs and Spud used a sack to cover his head. Despite a lot of thrashing about, Mr Campbell was well and truly trussed up.

'Like a chicken!' woofed Star, dusting her paws off and eyeing Kenneth Soop.

'You next,' she growled.

With the guard dogs out of action, Ben sprinted to the oven and hauled open the door. A wall of heat hit him, but he ventured inside none the less, shielding his face with his arm. *But . . . where was Lara?* Sophie and Ollie joined their brother.

'Oh no! Lara's melted!' cried Ollie.

In a modern day Wild West showdown, Maximus Cortex and Kenneth Soop eyed each other warily from three metres apart. Neither blinked. Soop's caterpillar moustache twitched and danced, scurrying around his top lip in agitation.

Mr Dewitt had entered the room.

'Activate the Cloud Maker,' shouted Soop, moustache still twitching, eyes fixed on Cortex.

'My pleasure,' nodded the old head teacher, slightly irritated by the arrival of unwanted guests.

'But the roof is closed!' shouted Professor Cortex. 'You'll create an indoor typhoon. Anything could happen!'

'Exactly,' sneered Soop, nodding again to Mr Dewitt.

The Cloud Maker exploded into life, just as Lara leapt from the top of the oven, a fraction too late to stop the old man from pressing the red button. There was an agonizing yell as Lara's teeth sank into Soop's leg. Streaks of lightning shot up towards the darkened sky. The telltale stink of burnt chicken signalled that yet more snot had been evaporated. The rays hit the glass ceiling and had nowhere to go. Dark clouds began to swirl around the dome and huge raindrops pelted down indoors. Dewitt had taken his cane to Lara. Three hearty whacks on the snout had caused her jaws to open and Soop was away. The exhausted Spy Dog welcomed the rain, the drops hissing as they hit her singed fur. Thunderclouds swirled around and Lara dodged a bolt of lightning.

Lara looked around, desperately trying to locate the crooks. Through the commotion, she spied Dewitt and Soop standing by a large container. The old head teacher slipped the bolt on the side of the crate, the doorway falling open with a shuddering thud to reveal hundreds of cooped-up chickens. The old man leant in and flexed his cane. Immediately, the chickens exploded hysterically from the crate – a cloud of feathers and claws adding to the overall mayhem. They could easily get away in the confusion now!

Lara's head hurt, partly from thinking and partly from the baseball bat. *I love catching baddies*, she thought, *but this indoor storm is too dangerous*. Another flash of lightning lit the dome and her decision was made. *The safety of the children is paramount*. Lara had no choice. She ushered the children out of the building.

By the time the police appeared, everyone was drenched and Kenneth Soop and Mr Dewitt had long since gone. Lara had cooled off sufficiently, pleased that the hot flush had passed. Somehow they'd all survived the storm. Professor Cortex was determined that there would not be another one, and had already set about dismantling the Climacta-sphere 2015. From time to time he'd let out small wondrous gasps and scribble something down in his notebook.

'Soop sure was evil,' murmured Professor Cortex, 'but there's no doubt he's a genius too.'

17. Unfinished Business

One month later . . .

The sun blazed down from a clear cobalt-blue sky. The air was thick and still, with not even a hint of breeze. Life was getting back to normal in Brickfield, the dark cloud that hung over the town for so long had become all but a distant memory. There was a carnival feel to Brickfield Primary's summer sports day. Agent GM451 (semi-retired) lay back on her striped deckchair. As a familiar face in these parts, she was something of a local celebrity: the village's best-kept secret. Lara sighed contentedly, glancing at her watch. *Soon be time to start the next race* – an honour that had been bestowed upon her in recent years.

Spud and Star returned, yapping and giggling,

124

both of them sporting a third-place sticker. The pups had just participated in the three-legged race, although they had argued it was unfair because they had twice as many legs to trip over. Ollie had disappeared to get some food, tempted by the smell of sizzling sausages.

Mrs Cook looked on nervously. Mr Cook was jogging up and down the grass verge – 'limbering up', as he had referred to it. The parents' race had been what Mr Cook had been training towards for months now. Mrs Cook didn't care whether he won or not, just as long as he reached the end in one piece.

Ollie ambled around the field among the various food stalls. A man dressed as an ice cream was handing out leaflets and a little further up a food van was serving burgers. Ollie looked wistfully at his pocket money; he didn't have quite as much as he'd thought. He knew he could go back and ask Mum or Dad, but they were right over the other side of the track, and there were already plenty of people queuing up. His tummy rumbled. If he had to wait much longer, he'd be starving.

Looking up, Ollie spied an old ice-cream van, but this one seemed to be selling . . . fried chicken. The van was parked up slightly behind the others, and appeared a little shabby. The paintwork was peeling and the windows were thick with grime. There was a large plastic chicken drumstick lying across the roof, with the letters 'k. nuggets' scrawled across it in black paint. Importantly, however, there was no one waiting to be served, so the little boy shrugged and walked over to take a closer look.

Lara took her place by the start line and pointed the starting-pistol towards the cloudless sky. Mr Cook was already crouching in one of the middle lanes, coiled like a rusty spring in anticipation of the bang. Either side of him were several mums who had kicked off their flip-flops, a dad who'd just removed his suit jacket and a rather wobbly-looking lady who might have drunk too much pop. Mrs Cook crossed her fingers. She could hardly bear to watch.

There were two men inside the van, accompanied by a huge dog that looked as if it had entered the fancy-dress competition. It seemed caked in make-up and wore a stupid hat, almost as if it were in disguise.

Glad he's got into the spirit of things, thought Ollie.

The first man was the oldest-looking man Ollie had ever seen. He appeared to be sleeping, a flat cap pulled down covering half his face. The second man was an extremely tall figure dressed in thin, black drainpipe trousers and a black polo-neck jumper. He looked a bit like a daddy-long-legs. He unscrewed a tall silver flask and took a sip of something, before wiping his moustache with his sleeve, leaving a silver trace. As Ollie approached the window, he turned round to face him.

Ollie gasped and took a step back. The man's face was hidden behind dark glasses and a baseball cap was pulled down tight. His long, spindly fingers splayed against the countertop, revealing breadcrumbs underneath his fingernails. He leant forwards, his breath reeking of chicken. Ollie knew exactly who he was.

'What can I get you?' smiled the man, his voice anything but welcoming.

Ollie had suddenly lost his appetite and he knew that he should find Mum and Dad.

'Err . . . I don't have any money,' the little boy stammered, edging further away.

'That's OK,' the spindly man continued, 'the nuggets are free.' He then held out a white polystyrene carton with one hand, before dolloping a dozen nuggets into it with his other. He handed them over with a withering look at the small boy in front of him, and suddenly snapped.

'I'm not in the soup business any more!' spat the man formerly known as Ken Soop. 'My life's work is gone, no doubt lying in pieces in some top-secret government laboratory! I'm finished, THANKS TO YOU AND YOUR INTERFERING PETS!'

Ollie turned to run, and bumped straight into the large dog with the scary eyes. Mr Campbell placed a large paw on Ollie's shoulder and growled menacingly.

'Let's see how Maximus Cortex likes losing something – or *someone* – important to him!' Ken Nuggets laughed, but he wasn't smiling.

BANG!

The starting-pistol fired and Dad sprinted off like a tortoise. The crowd cheered as the competitors rounded the bend. Spud, Star, Lara, Sophie, Ben and Mum all shouted words of encouragement. Dad was doing OK and even overtook one of the ladies carrying her flip-flops in one hand and holding her skirt in the other. The race was neck-and-neck as the runners entered the final straight. Mr Cook was now up to second place and was gaining on first. The pups were just starting to believe Dad could actually win when . . . he veered off the track sharply and carried on running in completely the wrong direction. Instead of racing for the finish, he ran right off the grass track, and appeared to be heading for the food stalls.

'What's wrong? Where's Dad going?' gasped Sophie, craning her head round to see.

'Maybe he's hungry,' suggested Ben half-heartedly.

'Something's wrong,' barked Lara, her spy-sense starting to tingle.

'Where's Ollie?' asked Mum, the panic starting to rise in her voice.

'There he is!' barked Star, racing after Mr Cook, who had already spotted Ollie struggling in the distance with the enormous guard dog.

Ollie was the smallest of the Cook family but also the bravest. He stamped on top of Mr Campbell's paw and the Great Dane let out a yowl, allowing the boy to squirm free of his grip.

'Grab him, you fool!' shouted Ken Nuggets, having decided a change of name would help him go unrecognized.

Ollie was also top of the 'lightning-fast'

category. He raced in the direction of Mr Cook, who was closing the gap rapidly. Mr Campbell hopped around on three paws, evidently in great pain.

Ken Nuggets realized he'd missed his chance. The boy had escaped. He banged his fists in frustration on the serving hatch, leaving a small pile of breadcrumbs.

'It wasn't the boy I wanted anyway,' he snarled. 'It was those dratted dogs!'

Leaping into the driver's seat, he slammed his foot on the accelerator and the van lurched forward.

18. Playing Ketchup

While Lara's legs no longer moved quite as fast as Spud's and Star's, her mind was still super speedy. The rest of the Cook family sprinted in the direction of Ollie, where all the excitement appeared to be taking place. Instead, GM451 used her years of experience and made her way directly to the park gate . . . *Where all the action is likely to be heading . . .*

Sure enough, the battered van roared across the grass, thick plumes of choking diesel smoke billowing out of its exhaust. Mr Cook was the first to reach Ollie. The two of them gave each other a relieved hug. Ollie grinned.

'Crumbs, Dad – that was quick!'

Dad brushed off the breadcrumbs on Ollie's shoulder.

'Crumbs, indeed. I think our friend Mr Soop

has developed a taste for chicken nuggets.' Star and Ben were the next to arrive, followed by Sophie and Spud. The two pups looked at each other knowingly. *He's back . . .*

Mrs Cook was the last to join the group.

'Come on,' she said, jangling the car keys, 'he needs stopping once and for all.' Everyone looked at her, slightly shocked. Mum was usually so sensible. 'He's cost Dad a gold medal!'

'To the Cook-mobile,' instructed Dad, racing off towards their old estate car.

'Cool,' said Ben, not quite able to believe it.

Lara dug her claws into the bark of the oak tree and grimaced, her paws scrabbling to reach the higher branches. Dogs were not meant to climb trees . . . *Or chimneys! But then again, I'm no ordinary dog*. The clapped-out van was rapidly approaching, and Lara knew that she was only going to get one shot at this. *What's new?*

Ken Nuggets gripped the steering wheel and gritted his teeth. He might have failed this time, but he intended to be back. Those dogs needed to be taught a lesson. Mr Dewitt snored.

Lara curled her paws around the underside of the branch and pulled herself along, edging further across the exit to the park. *Phew, made it — just in time!*

Nuggets looked in his rear-view mirror and could see a car was hot on their tail. *Not for long.*

Swerving round the corner, he slammed on the brakes, screeching to a halt in the middle of the gateway to the park. Reaching down with an orange, spindly finger, Nuggets flicked a switch on the dashboard. The van spluttered and shook. A wave of grey sludge slopped out of the exhaust pipe and sprayed the road near the exit. Nuggets waited for a moment, just to check that the contents had been completely emptied, before restarting the engine and roaring off down the road. He failed to register the sound of four paws dropping softly on to the roof of the van.

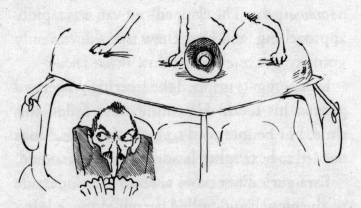

Mum was in the driving seat, a look of steely determination set on her face. The children held on to their seatbelts, as the car swung round the corner, straight into the pile of thick sludge. Before Mrs Cook could do anything to react, the car slowed to a standstill. Mum tried to reverse, but the gloop stuck to the wheels like chewing gum; they were going nowhere.

The family piled out of all five doors of the car to see the van disappearing up the road, a trail of smoke behind it.

'Is that Lara?' asked Sophie with surprise.

Squinting into the distance, they could just make out the black and white patches plastered to the roof. Spud and Star looked at each other with concern.

'I'll phone Professor Cortex,' said Dad.

Lara was hanging on for dear life, her ears firmly flattened to the side of her head and the wind whistling through her bullet hole. Now that she'd got herself into this precarious position, she wasn't entirely sure what to do next. She assessed the situation and two ideas came to mind. First she took off her collar and checked the Bluetooth connections.

Excellent, she yowled, remotely pairing her collar with the van's satnav. It was difficult in such a high wind, but she managed to change the destination of Nugget's satnav.

'At the next exit, turn left,' she heard from below. *And then there's the old ice-cream van's loudspeaker,* she thought. *That might come in handy too . . .*

Spud lifted up a paw and sniffed the gloop.

'Is that what I think it is?' he woofed.

Star nodded in agreement.

'Bogeys . . . chicken-flavoured.'

Everyone was out of the car, except Mum. Dad was behind the left rear wheel, pushing hard. Sophie and Ben were copying, on the right. Star and Spud were prancing around, up to their middles in bogey bog, barking wildly.

'Now!' yelled Dad.

Mum's foot hit the accelerator and the wheels spun, showering Dad in grey goo . . .

Ken Nuggets had slowed down from driving much too fast to merely too fast. He'd checked his mirrors and they seemed to be in the clear; no one was following.

'Looks like I'm the winner again!' he purred. 'The family has been given a nasty scare. Next time I'll finish the job.'

Nuggets had been careful to pre-programme the satnav with the coordinates of his next secret hiding place. He loved mimicking the lady's voice. 'At the next roundabout, take the third exit,' Lara heard him say.

Meanwhile, the Spy Dog was wrestling with the microphone wire linked to the speaker on the top of the van. She smiled a doggie smile as she heard Ken Nuggets arguing with the satnav.

'Are you sure?' he bellowed. 'Next left takes us into the town. Are you certain that's the quickest route?' As usual, he wanted to do it his way.

Lara spied the police station ahead. 'In one hundred metres, you have reached your destination,' soothed the female satnav.

Nuggets raged again. 'I don't think so, lady,' he yelled.

The van approached the police station. 'Destination reached,' announced the satnav.

The device was thrown from the window and Lara nearly fell off the roof as Nuggets realized his mistake and floored the accelerator. The engine thundered in complaint and black smoke belched out of the back of the van. Lara put the microphone to her lips and barked her loudest bark. Her normal bark carried a long way. Her magnified microphone bark was enough to wake up the whole town.

A burly policeman ran out of the station, rubbed his eyes

in disbelief and jumped in his car in hot pursuit. He knew Lara. She was the reason the police station had been reduced from fifteen officers to one. In fact, a runaway food van was the first crime he'd seen in months!

Lara knew it was only a matter of time. *My priority has to be a safe landing*, she thought as the roads whizzed by. The van was slow and the siren was getting closer. *I know that Nuggets, or Soop, will be panicking*. She saw the crossroads

138

approaching and noticed the red light was showing. The police car was gaining. *I doubt we're going to stop*, she thought.

A lorry was approaching from the right. RED TOMMY'S KETCHUP it said on the side.

The lorry driver glanced at the green traffic light and continued. Ken Nuggets glanced at the red traffic light and continued.

Lara's eyes grew wide as she realized what was about to happen. She threw herself off the roof of the van in the nick of time, landing on a grass verge and tumbling over several times. There was pain in her left shoulder and her right paw was limp.

But I'm breathing!

She lay there panting, waiting for the collision.

19. The Price of Sunshine

Kenneth swerved, but by then it was too late. The van ploughed into the side of the tomato-sauce lorry, piercing the trailer and flooding the carriageway with thick red ketchup. Ken found himself upside-down, floundering among a saucy sea of tomato. The driver of the tanker adjusted his cap and climbed down from the safety of his cab.

Ken Nuggets scrambled out of the van window. He was in shock.

'I'm dying,' he said. 'Look at me, covered in blood.'

Lara had righted herself, although she still didn't feel quite 'right'. She really was covered in blood. She limped towards the stricken baddie and sniffed. *I'd get cleaned up, mate, before Spud arrives. He loves tomato sauce.*

The police officer stepped forward and looked Nuggets in the eye.

'It's you,' he said. 'We've heard all about your escapades. Brickfield's most wanted. First soup, then nuggets, eh? Well, it's porridge for you from now on. You'll be going to prison for a very long time.'

As the baddies were led away, the policeman turned to Lara. He carefully undid his badge and placed it in the palm of his hand.

'I think this should be yours,' he smiled gratefully. 'Without you, Brickfield wouldn't be the safe and happy place it is.'

Lara's chest swelled with pride as the officer attached his sergeant's badge to her collar. *Now that's what I call a really 'smart' tag*, beamed Lara.

The Cook household was contented that evening for the first time in days. Professor Cortex had been with them for most of the afternoon. Spud and Star dozed somewhere in Ollie's room, snuggled among the piles of clothes and toys. A couple of feathers lay on top of the cupboard, a silent reminder of recent adventures. Spud twitched, dreaming of nuggets and soup.

The children and the professor were in the lounge. For once, the television was off and they were discussing the mission. Ben's laptop was open so that Lara could contribute, tapping the letters with a pencil. Other than a few bald patches, she had recovered well from being baked ('half-baked' as Dad kept saying) and falling off a burger van.

Sophie was explaining it to Ollie one more time.

'Soop was actually very clever. If you think about it, the ability to create clouds is genius.'

'Oh completely,' agreed Professor Cortex. 'And so simple! He'd realized that chicken sneezes contain a special enzyme, Omega 34, that coagulates with trace elements of atmospheric neon to create longevity of precipitation . . .'

Sophie decided to butt in.

'What that actually means, Ollie, is that there is a special ingredient in chicken snot that, if you spray it into the air, makes black clouds.'

'Quite,' nodded the scientist. 'Rather well put, young lady.'

'So he needed thousands of chickens. And when the chickens couldn't sneeze any more they became soup,' added Ben.

'And he added "down thyme" to the soup to make it addictive,' reminded Cortex. 'So he had the ultimate evil plot. A complete cycle. He created bad weather that made people sad. Sad people always reach for chicken soup. Once they tasted it, they wanted more . . . and so on and so on.'

'What about his sidekick, Mr Dewitt?' asked Ollie.

'My very old head teacher,' said Maximus Cortex, shaking his head sadly. 'Not evil. Just misguided. Soop needed somebody who knew about chickens. He didn't have any friends or anyone he could trust, so he tracked down Mr Dewitt and sort of roped the old man in. I guess the old head teacher just wanted to "Dewitt" his way one more time. He's back in the old folks' home. A different one. A caring care home. And he likes it because they give him egg-and-cress sandwiches. Every day.'

'Why didn't Soop use his big brain to do good?' asked Ollie innocently.

'That, Master Oliver, is the billion-dollar question,' sighed Professor Cortex.

'The multi-biLLION $ question,' tapped Lara. They waited while she pecked at the keyboard with the pencil held tightly in her mouth. 'Found SooP's laptop. SEEMs he had bigga Plan?'

'Yeeees,' nodded the professor, puffing out his cheeks. 'This, kids, is the bit you don't know. As GM451 says, we discovered Soop's laptop and found elaborate plans that go way beyond Brickfield. We were just an experiment! The first phase of his mission for global domination. Once he had proved his system worked, he was going to create black clouds over the whole of the country.'

'*Permanent* doom and gloom?' asked Sophie, creasing her brow.

'And then the world!' cooed the professor, eyes like globes.

Lara started tapping and all eyes went back to the laptop. 'HE was going to sell Sunny Days.'

'GM451 is absolutely correct. His big plan

wasn't soup at all. Once the country was under a black cloud, he was going to reveal himself as the master "weather changer". He figured we'd be so desperate for sunny days that we'd pay for them.'

'1 BILLion per sunny day' typed Lara on the laptop.

'Genius,' gasped Ben. 'I mean, *evil*. But genius,' he said, correcting himself before he sounded too impressed. 'And where is Soop now?'

'Somewhere where we needn't worry about him,' smiled the professor. 'A good lesson for you all. Crime doesn't pay. Thanks to Lara, the sun is shining once more.'

Lara nodded. *Baddies always get their just desserts.* She didn't need chicken soup to feel good. *I have my family.* She licked at one of her bald patches, another souvenir of a mission accomplished.

The high-security prison was in complete darkness as the clocks struck midnight. Overhead, a large black cloud began to rain, gently at first, before starting to pour. There was another storm brewing . . .

YOUR STORY STARTS HERE

If you love **BOOKS** and want to **DISCOVER** even more stories go to **www.puffinbooks.com**

- Amazing adventures, fantastic fiction and laugh-out-loud giggles
- Brilliant videos starring your favourite authors and characters
- Exciting competitions, news, activities, the Puffin blog and SO MUCH more . . .

Puffin's off to take a peek
www.puffinbooks.com

It all started with a Scarecrow

Puffin is over seventy years old.
Sounds ancient, doesn't it? But Puffin has never been
so lively. We're always on the lookout for the next big
idea, which is how it began all those years ago.

Penguin Books was a big idea from the mind of
a man called Allen Lane, who in 1935 invented
the quality paperback and changed the world.
**And from great Penguins, great Puffins grew,
changing the face of children's books forever.**

The first four Puffin Picture Books were hatched in 1940 and the
first Puffin story book featured a man with broomstick arms called
Worzel Gummidge. In 1967 Kaye Webb, Puffin Editor, started the
Puffin Club, promising to **'make children into readers'**.
She kept that promise and over 200,000 children became devoted
Puffineers through their quarterly instalments of *Puffin Post*.

Many years from now, we hope you'll look back and
remember Puffin with a smile. **No matter what your age
or what you're into, there's a Puffin for everyone.**
The possibilities are endless, but one thing is for sure:
whether it's a picture book or a paperback, a sticker book
or a hardback, **if it's got that little Puffin
on it – it's bound to be good.**

www.puffinbooks.com